11.99

Supernatural Stories

~ ⬮⬮ ~

13 Tales of the Unexpected

EDITED BY *Jean Russell*

ORCHARD BOOKS

A DIVISION OF FRANKLIN WATTS, INC.

New York and London

First American edition 1987
Copyright © 1987 by Orchard Books
All rights reserved. No part of this book may be reproduced or transmitted in any
form or by any means, electronic or mechanical, including photocopying, recording or by any information storage or retrieval system, without permission in
writing from the Publisher.
Orchard Books
A Division of Franklin Watts, Inc.
387 Park Avenue South, New York, NY 10016

The following stories are reprinted from *The Magnet Book of Strange Tales*,
copyright © 1980 Methuen Children's Books Ltd., 11 New Fetter Lane,
London EC4P 4EE: "The Whistling Boy"; "Mr. Hornet and Nellie Maggs";
"The Demon Kite"; and "Just a Guess."

The following stories were reprinted by permission from *The Magnet Book of
Sinister Stories*, copyright © Methuen Children's Books Ltd: "The Dollmaker";
"Miss Hooting's Legacy"; "Black Dog"; "Billy's Hand"; "Spring-heeled Jack";
"The Book of the Black Arts"; "The Parrot"; "The Boy's Story"; and
"Welcome, Yule".

"Miss Hooting's Legacy" copyright © 1982 Joan Aiken Enterprises Ltd.

The text of this book is set in 12 point Garamond
Manufactured in The United States of America
Book design by Sylvia Frezzolini
10 9 8 7 6 5 4 3 2 1

Library of Congress Cataloging-in-Publication Data
Magnet book of sinister stories. Selections Supernatural stories.
1. Supernatural—Juvenile fiction. 2. Children's stories, English.
[Supernatural—Fiction. 2. Short stories] I. Russell, Jean, b. 1939.
II. Magnet book of strange tales. Selections. 1987. III. Title.
PZ5.S963 1987 [Fic] 87-7881
ISBN 0-531-05723-2
ISBN 0-531-08323-3 (lib. bdg.)

Contents

The Dollmaker

꩜

BY ADÈLE GERAS

EVERYONE WHO LIVED IN BURTON BRIDGE KNEW AVRIL CLAY.
The children called her Auntie Avril. She was a small, unre-
markable woman, given to wearing unsuitable hats (ruched
velvet or massed flower petals) in all weathers. She lived in a
neat little cottage house on Elmford Lane and her garden was
full of tiny stone statues in unexpected places: not gnomes, but
squirrels, birds, hedgehogs and even a stone deer. How she fits
them into that pocket handkerchief of a garden, her neighbors
used to say, we'll never know. She loved children. She said so
herself. "Oh, I do love the kiddies, bless their hearts!" she would
exclaim whenever she saw them playing on the swings in the
park, or walking to school. The women shook their heads over
the coffee cups and whispered: "Such a shame that she never
married and had children of her own. Ever so fond of them, she
is. Such a pity."

It was a pity. No one knew it, no one suspected it because
after all, you don't go blurting these things out to everyone, but

1

being childless meant, for Avril Clay, walking around with a wound hurting somewhere where no one could see it. A constant pain, that bit into the very corners of her soul.

"She's so good with her hands." That was another thing they said about her, and it was true. Every jumble sale, school fair, Christmas bazaar or bring-and-buy for miles around would be filled with the things she had made: jam and chutney and lavender bags and quilts for dolls and pajama cases in the shape of bunny rabbits—there seemed to be nothing she couldn't turn her hand to.

"Miss Clay," the vicar used to say when confronted with her offerings, "that's a real labor of love."

On the first and third Wednesday of every month, Avril held a dolls' hospital in her home. Girls sat in her front parlor, clutching their broken darlings, and one by one they would be called into the workroom at the back of the house (in turn, just like a proper doctor's office) and Auntie Avril, wearing a flowered nylon smock, would look and diagnose and prescribe and place the dismembered creature on a shelf full of others like it.

"She'll be ready next week, dear," she'd say "good as new. Don't worry your little head about it anymore. Will you send the next person in as you leave, please? Thank you."

Ruth went into the workroom and looked down at the floor.

"Hello, Ruth dear," said Avril. "Come and sit down and show me what's the matter. Don't be shy."

Ruth sat down.

"Have a dolly mixture, love," Avril continued. "Dolly mixtures for dolls' hospital. I think that's appropriate, don't you?" She laughed, and Ruth gave a timid half-smile.

"Her head's come off," she said "and I can't seem to get it on."

"Let's have a look." Avril took the doll. "Oh, what a beauty she is, isn't she? Aren't you lucky? Eh? Such a lucky girl. Hasn't she got lovely hair, though? I don't think I've seen such hair for

2

ages. Marvelous, like a forest in autumn." Avril stroked the hair with greedy fingers. "She'll be ready next week, dear. You can call in any day after Tuesday. I'm always in in the afternoon."

"Thank you very much, Auntie Avril." Ruth stood up to go, and then blushed.

"Please may I go to the toilet?"

"Yes, of course, dear. First on the right at the top of the stairs. Will you send my next customer in on your way?"

"Yes, of course. And thank you."

Ruth waited until the door had shut behind Sandra and then went upstairs. She had no intention of going anywhere near the toilet. That was an excuse. She was going to look at *The Room.* They all called it that, everyone she knew who had been to Auntie Avril's. Angela was the only one who had ever seen inside it. She had told Ruth:

"It's upstairs next to the bathroom. You should have a look in there. It's really . . . I don't know . . . peculiar."

"What's in there?" Ruth had asked.

"Only dolls and things. Nothing scary, but I don't know . . . it gave me the creeps."

Ruth opened the door. It was a very small room, only a storeroom, really. There was a table pushed up against the window. On the walls there were hooks: hundreds of them, and hanging from the hooks were arms and legs and even bald dolls' heads with empty eye sockets, dangling in such a way as to make them seem alive, like bits of very small children. There was a shelf stacked with limbless bodies, plastic torsos waiting. Waiting to be made whole. Another shelf had small wigs balanced on rows and rows of little sticks. A large cookie tin lay open on the table, and Ruth went to look into it and drew back quickly. That's horrible, she thought, and then: how silly I am. It's only eyes . . . bits of plastic and glass, that's all. But the way they stared up at her, hard and unblinking, and the way they just seemed about to roll

3

around, or move, and all their different colors. . . . She left the room and closed the door behind her.

Later, she said to Angela: "I went up there. To the Room. I didn't think it was so bad. The eyes were a bit creepy. But it's only bits of dolls, after all. She couldn't mend our dolls if she didn't have any spare parts, could she?"

Angela said: "I suppose not. But all those legs and arms and things, just hanging there. I was in there for quite a long time. I tell you, after a bit they begin to look human in a funny kind of way. Especially the hands. Everything seemed . . . I can't describe it . . . as if it was going to move the minute I left, or as if it had just stopped moving when I went in."

"Are you going to come with me when I collect Meg?"

"O.K." said Angela. "When are you going?"

"Thursday. Jackie and Sandra are going then, too."

"Then we can all go straight from school. What's wrong with Jackie's doll? I know Sandra's brother broke the arms off her Alice."

"Jackie's doll had her legs squashed. Both smashed to pieces. Someone dumped a chest-of-drawers down on top of her when they were moving."

"Is that Elaine? That doll with the marvelous eyes? The one she got from America?"

"Yes," said Ruth. "I've never seen a doll with eyes like that. Kind of halfway between blue and mauve."

"The thing about them is, they look real. Not like doll's eyes at all. I wish I could get one like that."

"Fat chance, around here."

Ruth's mother said: "I see Auntie Avril mended Meg for you. That's good."

"Yes, I suppose so." Ruth sighed.

4

"What do you mean, you suppose so? You know how fond you are of that doll. Aren't you pleased to have her back in one piece?"

"Yes, I am. Of course I am. But she's different. . . ."

"No, she's not. She looks exactly the same to me."

Ruth shook her head. "She's not the same. Her hair's not the same."

"What's the matter with it?"

"It used to be silky," said Ruth. "Don't you remember? And that lovely color, like chestnuts, and now it's all nylonish and stiff and just an ordinary brown."

"Let's have a look." Ruth's mother looked closely at the doll's head. "It seems exactly the same to me, I promise you. Auntie Avril wouldn't have needed to touch the hair."

"She didn't need to touch the hair at all. But she has."

"Why, though?"

"I don't know why. I just know that this hair is awful. I think she stole Meg's hair, that's what."

"Oh, don't be silly, Ruth. Whatever would she want to do a thing like that for? It's very naughty to say such things about anyone, let alone poor old Avril. Don't let me hear you say that again. Stealing indeed!"

Ruth didn't answer. She went upstairs and sat on her bed and looked at Meg. If Auntie Avril *had* stolen Meg's hair, where was it now? On that shelf in the storeroom? Why? Why had Auntie Avril done it? Ruth shivered.

Avril was working. Remove. Replace. Sort. Cut. Glue. She was humming to herself. Somewhere, deep inside where the Pain always was, she felt small stirrings of joy, of anticipation, of pleasure, such as she imagined a woman must feel when she was aware, for the first time, of a living child growing within her.

5

Avril worked late. Choose. Change. Mold and twist. Make and yearn. All through the night.

Jackie and Sandra were playing in Jackie's bedroom. Jackie said: "You know Ruth's doll, Meg? Well, I saw her the other day and her hair is different. Meg's hair, and you say Alice's skin is all funny, and just look at Elaine's eyes."

Elaine, of the famous lilac-colored eyes, all the way from America, was lying on the floor. Sandra picked her up. Her eyes were a flat, dull blue.

"Gosh," Sandra said, "they are different. I can see it quite clearly. We were all dead jealous of your Elaine's eyes. Did you tell your mother?"

"Yes, and my dad. They thought I was crazy. Swore blind that the eyes were the same as they always were. Said I had too much imagination, and anyway. . . ." Jackie paused.

"What?"

"They said that as it was the legs of my doll that were broken, they were the bits that would have been replaced. She'd not have needed to go near the eyes, would she?"

"No, she wouldn't. But she did, didn't she?"

"Yes."

"But why?"

"I don't know. Your Alice only needed her arms fixed and now you say her skin is all funny. Actually. . . ."

"What?"

"I don't see how she could fiddle with a doll's skin, do you? I mean, she couldn't just peel it off, could she?"

"I know you don't believe me," Sandra said "but it's true. I don't know how she did it. Or what for. But Alice had a special skin. A special sort of color. I always thought she looked more . . . alive, more real, because of it. It had a kind of glow to it as if. . . ." Sandra broke off, unable to find the right words. Then

6

she said: "As if she were a real person. It even felt softer than a doll's skin normally does."

"Did you tell your parents?"

"No."

"Why not?"

"They wouldn't believe me. I don't even think you and Ruth and Angela believe me."

"I do," said Jackie. "At least, I think I do. But what can we do about it? We can't go back to Auntie Avril and complain, can we?"

"No." Sandra shook her head.

"Then what can we do?"

"Forget about it, I suppose. But I do think it's odd, all the same."

A notice went up outside Avril Clay's house in Elmford Lane. It said: "There will be no dolls' hospital for the next two months, because of family problems."

The children told their mothers, who speculated over the coffee cups. What problems? If it came right down to it, what family? Wasn't there a sister in Canada? No, not a sister. A cousin, that's right. But in Canada. Had anyone seen Avril lately? And why had she missed the Farlow Road High School fair for the first time in years? Should we call and see if she's all right? She may be ill. But somehow, no one felt they knew her well enough to intrude, and anyway she couldn't be ill, because Mrs. Webb had seen her at the store, and Jane and Sally had waved to her the other day in the park, they'd said, and she was very cheery. Her hat was covered in pink blossoms, apparently. That doesn't sound like someone who's sick, now does it? All the same. . . .

Avril worked at night, behind drawn curtains. Every night. It was the hardest, most delicate work she had ever done. In her

7

heart, the years of wanting and hurting and longing were like a machine powering her fingers, driving her skillful hands. She never stopped. Choose. Cut. Sew. Make. Bind. Mold. And, at last, behind drawn curtains, it was finished. A labor of love indeed. A labor of more than love.

The dolls' hospital reopened. There was no more speculation. Avril told everyone she met that Hazel, her cousin's child, was coming to live with her. The cousin, poor woman, had died, far away in Canada, and who could the poor child live with but Avril?

"I'm very sorry for my cousin, of course," she would say to anyone who would listen. "Losing her husband, and now this . . . but I'll be so happy to have Hazel. It'll be just like having a child of my own. And you know how I love the kiddies!"

The women nodded, and talked of blessings in disguise, and ill winds blowing no good, and Hazel's loss being Avril's gain.

Ruth and Jackie and Sandra spread the word among their friends. Those girls who took their dolls to the hospital and sneaked upstairs to look into the Room, reported that it was always locked. No way of finding out what had happened to Meg's hair and Elaine's eyes. As for Alice's skin, well, most of the girls concluded that Sandra had only made that up so as not to be left out. Sandra, however, knew she hadn't and sometimes at night, she dreamed of Auntie Avril, peeling away the layers of Alice's soft skin with her bare hands.

"That's Hazel, look. Over there." Ruth pointed.

"Where?" Jackie craned her neck to see.

"I can see her," said Angela.

"She's awfully pretty," Sandra added. "Let's go over and talk to her."

"She's only a first-year student, though," said Ruth. "Won't she think it's a bit peculiar if we all come up to her at once?"

8

"Well, we don't have to talk to her, do we?" said Jackie. "Just go a little closer. Have a look. She looks nice."

"Yes, lovely," said Sandra. "I'm going."

They walked over to the bench on which Hazel was sitting with her new friends. Ruth stared at her, fascinated. Her hair, in the September sunshine, shone like chestnuts, all the color of the leaves in autumn. Her skin glowed as if it were lit from within. Sandra thought: Alice's skin was just like that. I wish I could touch it and see . . . Hazel looked up. Jackie gasped and ran away. Ruth and Sandra ran after her.

"Whatever's wrong, Jackie? What's the matter?"

"Her eyes! Did you see them? Did you?"

"No, what was wrong with them?" said Angela.

"They're Elaine's eyes. That's what. She's got eyes like Elaine. Exactly the same."

"It's a coincidence, that's all," said Ruth.

"I don't believe it!" Jackie was shouting. "I just don't believe it. Look at her! Look at her hair and her skin! I think Auntie Avril stole bits from all our dolls, and probably from others as well, and made herself a person, that's what I think!"

"You're crazy."

"That's impossible. . . ."

"You'd better not go round saying that," said Angela quietly, "or people will think you're mad. Even if it's true. Especially if it's true. They will take you away if you say things like that. Really. Don't say it anymore."

And so the girls said nothing. But they knew. They never played with Hazel. If she came to the playground in the park, they left quickly and went to feed the ducks instead.

The Whistling Boy

BY JOHN GORDON

IT CAME TO A HEAD THE DAY THAT BONZO WATERED THE
garden.

"I was only trying to help," he said.

The others, gathered near the park gate, were laughing, as
they had been for some minutes. Several were even draped over
the low railing around the shrubbery, weak with the strain.

"How long did you say it took?" said Tom Jex, his great friend.

"Well it's only a small garden," said Bonzo.

"I know." Tom had quite often been in the garden even
though, if Bonzo's grandmother were there, they would be driven
out pretty quickly. It was more a yard than a garden, very tiny,
with an old wash-house along one side, and tall walls. The bit
that could be called a garden was a strip of earth along one side.
It was full of flowers—or had been.

"It only took two watering cans," said Bonzo.

"And how much weed killer did you put in?"

10

Bonzo's large, pink face took on a slightly redder shade. "Only what was left in the box," he said.

"But you told me you'd just opened a new one."

"Well, I mean," said Bonzo, "I only used what was left when I filled the second can."

There was a splutter from the railings.

"So you used it all?"

"Well, I suppose so."

"And how long," said Tom carefully, "did it take to show?"

"Oh, I don't know." Bonzo showed signs of wanting to change the subject. He gave the railings a shake to the great danger of the draped figures.

"I mean," Tom insisted, "did the flowers begin to droop right away?"

"Of course not!" Bonzo was indignant. He had been thoroughly misunderstood. "They didn't go brown until dinner time!"

There was a dull thud as two figures, like shot crows, fell from the railing and lay on the grass in the dusk, wheezing and rattling as they fought for breath.

"What did it look like next morning?" said Tom.

"Oh well, that's different, of course." Bonzo, having made his point that the disaster hadn't come about as quickly as everybody believed, was quite prepared to describe the dramatic outcome once again. "All their petals had dropped off and they'd all bent over. Most of them lay quite flat." He thought for a moment. Then he said, frowning as he tried to imagine it. "I should think that if you got a flame-thrower and gave them a good blast they would look a bit like that. You know, burned."

Tom doubled up and joined the others on the grass. They kicked and heaved and wheezed, but after a time the pain was not so great and they sat up.

"What about your mom?" said one of the others.

"Oh, she wasn't so bad. She laughed a bit." Bonzo's plump face was smiling benignly. He was pleased to have amused so many people. But then he frowned as though he had felt a twinge. "It's my Granny that's the trouble."

Tom knew very well what he meant. Bonzo's mother was very much like Bonzo himself, tall and plump and rather stately, never greatly troubled by anything. His father had died long before Bonzo could remember, and his grandmother had moved in. She was much smaller than her daughter but bullied her. She had hair of iron gray clamped close to her head like a helmet, steel-rimmed glasses, a downturned mouth and a voice that clattered like a box full of cutlery.

"She tried to catch me," he said, "but I ran out of the house and had dinner with my mom uptown."

Bonzo's mother worked in a shop on the Market Place and sometimes, in the holidays, he would go to a café with her for lunch. They both knew that the house was too uncomfortable for him with only his grandmother there.

It was getting dark. Across the park, shadows were thickening beneath the trees as though the darkness was growing upward to join the branches to the ground. A massive silence had descended over the whole town, bringing with it a kind of sadness. Tom looked at Bonzo. There was just enough light on his face to show that the sadness had crept into him and, with a kind of chill surprise, Tom felt what it was like to be Bonzo. In a moment he would put his friends behind him and wander away to the other side of the park, to the tiny house which his steelly grandmother had made into a cold prison.

He wished he could ask him to his own house; that would cheer him up. But it was too late. Instead, he said, "Tell you what."

Bonzo looked up. "What?"

"I'll walk home with you."

12

"That's not much of a tell-you-what."

They laughed and were still in a good mood when they reached Bonzo's house. It was in a jumble of narrow streets crowded close to the park but hidden from it by the tall trees. At the front the house was in darkness, but downstairs the curtains were slightly parted and Tom could see the pale glimmer of the plaster figure that stood on a little pedestal in the window. It was a barefoot boy standing with his hands in the pockets of his ragged trousers and with a floppy hat pushed to the back of his head.

"He's always happy, anyway," said Tom, feeling the gloom begin to descend once more on Bonzo.

"Do you reckon?"

"Well, he never stops whistling."

The boy had his head thrown back as he blew, and he obviously had no care in the world.

"I can't understand it," said Bonzo. There was no need for him to say any more; they both knew the whistling boy was one of his grandmother's possessions, and she had nothing to do with happiness.

As Bonzo pushed open the front door, Tom held the knocker to prevent it from rattling. They could hear voices from the room at the back, but with luck Bonzo would be able to get to bed without once more having to suffer his grandmother's wrath.

"See you tomorrow," said Tom.

"If I survive."

The door closed softly.

Next afternoon they were playing ball in the park, but not very well.

"You want to try throwing a bit faster, Bonzo," said one of his team.

"You can't get spin if you throw fast," he said.

"What spin?"

13

"The way I do it."

"That ball wasn't spinning. It floated."

"Like a balloon," said someone.

"You could read the maker's name on it," said someone else.

"And count the stitches."

Bonzo looked at them loftily. "Very funny," he said.

"Watch out," said Tom, trying to protect him, "you'll make him mad."

"He's gone red already."

"He'll go green in a minute."

"Like the Hulk."

"Bonzo the Hulk."

"Let's see your shirt split, Bonzo."

"His trousers are tight enough already."

It was getting worse. Tom broke in again. "He could beat any of you," he said. There were no challengers. "Any two of you."

Those who had been taunting Bonzo now lay on the grass as though the subject held no interest.

"Come on," said Tom to him. "They're not worth bothering with."

They wandered away together, and Bonzo, who had enjoyed playing ball in spite of everything, became silent. Tom looked at him. Bonzo was having a bad time. He was in trouble at home, and now his friends were making fun of him.

"Come and have tea at our house," he said suddenly.

Bonzo brightened but it was not because of the invitation. "No," he said. "You come around to mine." He saw Tom's surprise, and added quickly, "It's all right, my Gran's gone out."

The little house was quiet except for the hum of the canning factory at the end of the street. They went up to Bonzo's bedroom. It was very neat, and Bonzo was apologetic. "I used to have a battle scene on that chest of drawers," he said. "Tanks and airplanes. But she came and swept them all away."

14

"Not your mom."

"No. She said I could do it, but Gran came and did it when there was nobody at home. There was a fight about it and my mom said I could put 'em back, but I thought I'd better not."

"You're afraid of her." Tom could not resist it. "You're chicken."

"I ain't."

There was a long pause, and then Tom said something that soon he was to be sorry for. "Prove it."

Bonzo was no coward." All right," he said.

Tom knew it meant more trouble, and Bonzo had more than enough. "I didn't mean it," he said, and tried to restrain him, but it was too late. Bonzo had picked up something from the table beside his bed and was heading out of the room. All Tom could do was follow.

They clattered downstairs and into the front room. Bonzo went straight to the figure of the whistling boy.

"She's always polishing him," he said. He had a strange look on his face. It was almost savage. Something had come to the surface from beneath all the layers of his good nature, and Tom could do nothing about it. "She really treasures this." Bonzo was lifting the statue of the whistling boy from its pedestal.

"Careful." Tom was alarmed. "You'll break it."

"So what." It was a different Bonzo. His plump face was flushed and his dark eyes were feverish and hard. "She busted my airplanes, I'll bust her blasted boy." He thumped the figure on the carpet, but breaking it was not his intention. He still had in his hand the object he had picked up in his bedroom. It was a pencil box, and he opened it to spill out its contents.

"I've always wanted to do this." He picked up a felt pen. It was green, and he began stabbing it at the shining glaze of the boy's face. "Measles," he said. "Worse. Bubonic plague."

15

The spots multiplied, spreading to the arms and even the legs beneath the ragged edges of the trousers.

"Looks serious," said Tom.

"Fatal."

Bonzo put the green pen aside and picked up a brown one. He began drawing in a heavy mustache. Tom laughed, but his heart was not in it. It was not that he minded Bonzo defying his grandmother, it was more that there was something about the whistling boy he liked. He wore rags but didn't care. He had his bare feet thrust into grass and, as he gazed out into the world, he whistled.

"He doesn't look a bad old boy," he said as the rather girlish rosebud lips disappeared beneath Bonzo's pen. "I shouldn't think he'd mind dressing up."

"You reckon?" Bonzo looked up. The burst of activity had driven away some of his feverishness. "I always thought him and me could be friends." He was silent for a moment and then said, "If it wasn't for her." He stood up and lifted the plaster figure. "Come on then, Whistler, let's see what you look like on your platform."

The whistling boy was quite large and heavy, so they lifted him together. He had the face of a spotty, leering old man and they began to laugh.

"He looks a lot better like that," said Bonzo. "And I know some other people who could be improved."

"So do I," said Tom.

They were kneeling on the carpet drawing mustaches on each other when a shadow fell across them. They looked up. For a moment Tom thought the whistling boy was toppling from his pedestal, but then a rap on the glass drew his eyes beyond the boy to the window. The light was behind her, but there was no mistaking her shape or the glint of steel in her helmet of hair.

The window shook to a hailstorm of raps as her fury could

not be contained. Then she vanished. They heard her foot scrape on the step and a moment later her tread in the hallway.

The door swung back and she stood there, slightly bent, her head thrust forward. There was a mesh of fine wrinkles over her gray skin, and her mouth was pulled fiercely down at the corners. Her eyes glittered.

"Ha, my lad!" Her voice was sharp and full of triumph. "You don't get away with it this time!"

"I didn't damn well get away with it last time." The words were no more than a mutter, but Bonzo's daring made Tom go cold. He saw the old woman's lips vanish in a bunch of tight wrinkles, and then her voice came again in a kind of subdued shriek.

"Mary!" The large shape of Bonzo's mother appeared behind her. "Mary, did you hear what that boy said to me!"

"No, Mother."

"Filthy words, Mary! Filthy words!"

She advanced, and a faint smell of lavender came with her like the sweet odor of a venomous animal.

Tom began to move backward but Bonzo, in front of him, held his ground. Her head weaved slightly as though she was looking for a place to strike. Then she straightened.

"Come here, Mary." Her voice was less loud, but certain of victory. Her eyes remained fixed on Bonzo and, as his mother came forward, Tom risked a glance at the statue. The whistling boy's face was turned away from the old woman and she had not yet seen his decorations.

The voice grated again. "I want you to go to my purse in the sideboard drawer, Mary, and count the money."

The large, round face of Bonzo's mother was astonished. "Mother, what are you saying?"

"I'm saying, Mary, that your son cannot be trusted. He knows he's not supposed to come into this room. He knows because I

17

have told him over and over again that everything I treasure is kept in here. And yet he defies me and brings his thieving little friends into the house, and when I catch them red-handed he flings filthy words in my face!"

"Mother!"

The old woman had drawn herself rigidly straight. She clutched her handbag to her stomach. "Just look at them," she said. "There's guilt written all over their faces."

It was her first mistake, for Bonzo's mother, coming further into the room, at last saw them clearly. Her expression changed. "What on earth have you been doing?" she said. She seemed to find it difficult not to laugh.

"Nothing," said Bonzo innocently. He glanced at Tom. "Have we?"

But now they saw each other again, heavily spotted and with drooping mustaches.

"Well," Bonzo added, "nothing much."

She tried not to grin as she turned away. "There now, Mother, can't you see they've not done anything wrong?"

But the old woman had already sensed defeat on that score, and she was looking around sharply for a new line of attack. She darted forward with a speed that took them all by surprise.

"What about this then, Mary?" She had noticed the whistling boy askew on his pedestal. "They've been interfering with my personal property!"

She began to straighten the boy, but suddenly she lifted him clear and looked at him aghast.

"Look!" She held him out at arm's length. "Just look what they've done!"

Bonzo knew his mother's good humor could not withstand a fresh onslaught and he acted quickly.

"I can soon rub it off," he said. "Look."

He made a grab for the figure but his grandmother held on.

Bonzo's eagerness to put things right made him tug, and her dislike of him made her draw back quickly. There was a small rasping sound as the figure's arm snapped off.

For a long, cold moment there was not a movement in the room. The old woman was pale and had clamped her mouth tight. She gloried in her hatred and in the victory the accident had presented to her.

"I didn't mean it." Bonzo's voice was very small. The broken arm lay in his hand and he pushed it toward the figure. "I can fix it. I've got some stuff."

His mother came forward. "Let him do it," she said. "He's quite good at that sort of thing. And he does like the whistling boy; he's always said so."

The old woman did not answer. She snatched the broken piece from Bonzo's hand, turned quickly and left the room. His mother, as though she did not know what else to do, had taken out her handkerchief, licked it and was wiping the marks from his face.

She had only just begun when, from the yard at the back, there came a dull crash and then a pounding as something heavy was beaten against the flagstones.

Bonzo's mother kept on wiping until every mark had left his face. Tom was still rubbing at his own skin when the old woman's tread made them stop.

She stood in the doorway.

"You'll have a job to put him together, now, sonny lad," she said. "I've taken a hammer to him."

"Oh, Mother." The large figure of Bonzo's mother sagged. She spoke quite quietly. "Why did you have to do that?"

"Because I will not have him touch anything of mine. Nothing. He's just like his father. Useless. Wasting everybody's time."

"Mother!"

It was almost a wail, but the old woman advanced further into the room, pushing her daughter aside, and sat herself

19

heavily in a chair beside the dining table. She was breathing hard and her cheeks were bluish.

"It's no good, Mary. You should never have married that man. You know I never liked him. And now look what's happened. It's all his fault. All of it."

Bonzo's mother was crying, the tears running gently down her large cheeks.

Bonzo himself was almost in tears, but anger made him shout at his grandmother. "I hate you!" he yelled. "Everybody hates you!"

And then he ran, out of the front door into the street.

Tom hesitated, not knowing what to do. Bonzo's mother was silently weeping and the old woman's pinched face was saying bitterly, "And good riddance. Like father like son. May he never come back."

And then Tom could stand it no longer. He plunged out of the room and out of the house.

It was not until they had reached the marketplace that he caught up with Bonzo, and even then Bonzo kept his face turned away. Tom knew he had been crying as he ran.

They wandered aimlessly for a long while before Tom eventually persuaded him to come home to tea, but Bonzo would only do so after he had written a note and Tom had pushed it through the letter box.

"I don't want to worry her," he said. "She worries about everything."

Bonzo's own worries hung over him like a cloud all evening. They met the others in the park and, although the afternoon disagreement had been forgotten, nothing else they did aroused much excitement, and as dusk gathered they had been reduced to chasing each other through the shrubbery. Gradually they became widely separated, and the game expanded to encompass the entire

20

park. It became good fun to stalk a distant figure, track him down and catch him, and after a while they began to hunt in pairs, calling to each other in barks and yelps as they closed in on their prey.

Tom and Bonzo came together.

"What do you think?" said Tom.

"I saw one over there." Bonzo pointed toward a group of trees that stood alone in the grass. "Let's get him."

He was enjoying himself at last and Tom felt his own heart lift. "Right," he said. "You go that way. Whistle when you're in position."

They parted, loping across the darkening grass like a pair of wolves. Soon the copse was between them. Tom changed direction and crept toward it. He heard Bonzo's whistle and answered it. There were five large trees in the copse, standing roughly in a circle. Through them, Tom thought he could see Bonzo in the open on the far side, but he was not sure he could see anybody in the darkness at the center. He lay full length and looked along the grass. There was a dark shape in the middle. Their victim was simply sitting there, unaware he was trapped.

Bonzo on his side of the trees was crawling forward. He heard Tom's whistle and answered it. The figure crouching in the center paid no attention. The plan was working perfectly, and Bonzo forgot everything else.

Then they were each behind a tree trunk and ready to edge forward. The time for whistling had passed. Tom saw Bonzo come out into the open to begin his final dash and he also lunged from cover.

But suddenly there was nothing to aim for. Their victim had outwitted them. He had gone.

They pulled up short and then, away to one side, as though it had been one of themselves, came a low whistle. They were being mocked.

21

Together they ran toward the place, but as they did so a figure broke away, ran and twisted and was behind another trunk out of reach. They heard him laugh.

It happened again. Their dash was thwarted. They pulled up together, leaning against a tree, panting.

"Tell you what," said Bonzo, gasping, "I'm going to take my shoes and socks off."

"That's not a bad tell-you-what for once," said Tom.

Barefoot they ran much faster and quieter. They were very nearly the match for their tormentor, who was also unshod and whose shirt, like theirs, hung from his trousers and flapped like rags as he ran.

It became a three-way game. They chased each other, dodging and twisting among the five trees, hiding, giving a clue with a whistle, and then chasing to a new hiding place. It was getting very dark, but still the game went on, fast and furious, making them twist and weave as though in a dance.

Suddenly there was silence. One figure was in the middle again, daring the others. He stood with his hands in his pockets, his bare feet planted firmly in the grass, his head thrown back, and he whistled. The other two crept closer. They could hear each other panting but all they could see was the glimmer of their shirts.

They leapt. They grabbed limbs, heaved and rolled in the dust, and then they sat up.

"Got you," said Tom.

"It's me," said Bonzo. "You got me."

"Where's the other one, then?"

But he was gone. They searched and called out, but it was too dark to have any hope of finding him. After a while they put on their socks and shoes and wandered out of the park.

"That was good," said Bonzo. "I enjoyed that." As he got

closer to home, however, the shadows began to gather again and he fell silent.

"We'll have another game tomorrow night," said Tom. "Perhaps he'll be there."

"Maybe."

They stood outside Bonzo's door. He was reluctant to go in.

"Don't worry about it," said Tom. "She'll have got over it by now."

They both looked at the window beside the door. Behind the net curtain there should have been the glimmer of the whistling boy's pale face. There was nothing but darkness.

"She broke him up," said Bonzo. "There was no need for that."

The door was suddenly jerked wide. Both of them looked up, their mouths open. Bonzo's mother stood there.

"I heard you talking," she said. "Has anybody spoken to you?"

They shook their heads, not understanding. There was something strange about her.

"It's your Granny," she said. "She was taken ill just after you left. She's dead."

They stood there, all three, in the silent street. Tom remembered the blueness in the old woman's face and the catch in her breath after she had broken the whistling boy into pieces. Nobody spoke. And then, from somewhere in the park, the sound reached them. It must have been the boy they had just left. He whistled. He was still there, running barefoot in the dark. They listened. His whistle came once again, and then his laughter from deep among the trees.

Miss Hooting's Legacy

BY JOAN AIKEN

FOR WEEKS BEFORE COUSIN ELSPETH'S VISIT, MRS. ARMITAGE was, as her son Mark put it, "flapping about like a wet sheet in a bramble bush."

"What shall we do about the unicorn? Cousin Elspeth doesn't approve of keeping pets."

"But she can't disapprove of him. He's got an angelic nature —haven't you, Candleberry?"

Harriet patted the unicorn and gave him a lump of sugar. It was a hot day in early October and the family were having tea in the garden.

"He'll have to board out for a month or two at Coldharbour Farm." Mrs. Armitage made a note on her list. "And you," she said to her husband, "must lay in at least five cases of Glensporran. Cousin Elspeth will only drink iced tea with whisky in it."

"Merciful powers! What this visit is going to cost us! How long is the woman going to stay?"

"Why does she have to come?" growled Mark, who had been told to dismantle his homemade nuclear turbine, which was just outside the guest room window.

"Because she's a poor old thing and her sister just died, and she's lonely. Also, she's very rich, and if she felt like it, she could easily pay for you and Harriet to go to college, or art school, or something of that sort."

"But that's *years* from now!"

"*Someone* has to think ahead in this family," said Mrs. Armitage, writing down *Earl Grey tea, New face-towels* on her list. "And, Harriet, you are not to encourage the cat to come upstairs and sleep on your bed. It would be awful if he got into Cousin Elspeth's room and disturbed her. She writes that she is a very light sleeper."

"Oh, poor Walrus. Where *can* he sleep, then?"

"In his basket, in the kitchen. And, Mark, will you ask Mr. Peake to stay out of the guest bathroom for a few months? He's very obliging, but it always takes a long time to get an idea into his head."

"Well he *is* three hundred years old, after all," said Harriet. "You can't expect a ghost to respond quite as quickly as ordinary people."

"Darling," said Mrs. Armitage, to her husband, "some time this week, could you find a few minutes to hang up the big mirror that I bought at Dowbridges' sale? It's been down in the cellar for the last two months."

"Hang it, where?" said Mr. Armitage, reluctantly coming out of his evening paper.

"In the guest room, of course! To replace the one that Mark broke when his turbine exploded."

"I'll do it, if you like," said Mark, who loved banging in nails. "After all, it was my fault the other one got broken."

"And I'll help," said Harriet, who wanted another look at the new mirror.

She had accompanied her mother to the furniture sale, a couple of months ago, when three linen tablecloths, one wall mirror, ten flower pots, and a rusty pressure cooker had been knocked down to Mrs. Armitage for twelve pounds, in the teeth of spirited and urgent bidding from old Miss Hooting, who lived at the other end of the village. For some reason the old lady seemed particularly keen to acquire this lot, though there were several other mirrors in the sale. At eleven pounds ninety-nine, however, she ceased to wave her umbrella, and limped out of the sale hall, scowling, muttering, and casting angry glances at Mrs. Armitage. Since then she had twice dropped notes, in black spidery handwriting, through the Armitage letterbox, offering to buy the mirror, first for twelve pounds fifty, then for thirteen pounds, but Mrs. Armitage, who did not much like Miss Hooting, politely declined to sell.

"I wonder *why* the old girl was so keen to get hold of the mirror?" remarked Harriet, holding the jam jar full of nails while Mark tapped exploringly on the wall, hunting for reliable spots. The mirror was quite a big heavy one, about four feet long by two feet wide, and required careful positioning.

"It seems ordinary enough." Mark glanced at it casually. The glass, plainly quite old, had a faint silvery sheen; the frame, wooden and very worn, was carved with vine leaves and little grinning creatures.

"It doesn't give a very good reflection." Harriet peered in. "Makes me look frightful."

"Oh I dunno; about the same as usual, I'd say," remarked her brother. He selected his spot, pressed a nail into the plaster, and gave it one or two quick bangs. "There. Now another here. Now pass us the glass."

They heard the doorbell ring as Mark hung up the mirror, and

26

when, a few minutes later, they came clattering downstairs with
the hammer and nails and the step ladder, they saw their mother
on the doorstep, engrossed in a long, earnest conversation with
old Mrs. Lomax, Miss Hooting's neighbor. Mrs. Lomax was not
a close friend of the Armitage family, but she had once obligingly
restored the Armitage parents to their proper shape when Miss
Hooting, in a fit of temper, had changed them into ladybugs.

Odd things frequently happened to the Armitages.

"What did Mrs. Lomax want, Ma?" Harriet asked her mother
at supper.

Mrs. Armitage frowned, looking half worried, half annoyed.

"It's still this business about the mirror," she said. "Old Miss
Hooting had really set her heart on it, for some reason. Why
didn't she just *tell* me so? Now she has got pneumonia, she's
quite ill, Mrs. Lomax says, and she keeps tossing and turning,
and saying she has to have the mirror, and if not, she'll put a
curse on us by dropping a bent pin down our well. Perhaps, after
all, I had better let the poor old thing have it."

"Why? You bought it," said Harriet. "She could have gone on
bidding."

"Perhaps eleven pounds ninety-nine was all she had."

"There were other mirrors that went for less."

Mr. Armitage was inclined to make light of the matter. "I
don't see what dropping a bent pin into the well could do. I
expect she's delirious. Wait till she's better; then you'll find the
whole thing has died down, very likely."

Next day, however, the Armitages learned that old Miss
Hooting had died in the night.

"And not before it was time," said Mr. Armitage, "She must
have been getting on for a hundred. Anyway, that solves your
problem about the mirror."

"I hope so," said his wife.

"Now all we have to worry about is Cousin Elspeth. Did you

27

say she takes cubes of frozen tea in her whisky, or frozen whisky in her tea?"

"Either way will do, so long as the tea is Earl Grey. . . ."

Cousin Elspeth's arrival coincided with old Miss Hooting's funeral.

The funeral of a witch (or "old fairy lady" as they were always politely referred to in the Armitages' village, where a great many of them resided) is always a solemn affair, and Miss Hooting, because of her great age and explosive temper, had generally been regarded as the chairwitch of the village community. So the hearse, drawn by four black griffins and carrying a glass coffin with Miss Hooting in it, looking very severe in her black robes and hat, was followed by a long straggling procession of other old ladies, riding in vehicles of all kinds, from rickety perch phaetons with half the springs gone to moth-eaten flying carpets and down-at-the-wheel chariots.

Mark and Harriet would very much have liked to attend the ceremony, but were told firmly that, since the family had not been on very good terms with Miss Hooting, they were to stay at home and not intrude. They heard later from their friend Rosie Perrow that there had been a considerable fuss at the graveside, because Miss Hooting had left instructions that her coffin was not to be covered over until November 1, and the vicar had very strong objections to this.

"Specially as the coffin was made of glass," Rosie reported.

"I suppose he thought kids might come and smash it," said Mark.

"So they might. Miss Hooting wasn't at all popular."

Cousin Elspeth, when she arrived, was in a state of high indignation.

"Rickety, ramshackle equipages all along the village street, holding up the traffic! My taxi took twenty-eight minutes to get here, and cost me nine pounds eighty-three! Furrthermore, I am accustomed to take my tea at four-thirty preecisely, and it is now twelve meenutes past five!"

Cousin Elspeth was a tall, rangy lady, with teeth that Mr. Armitage said reminded him of the cliffs of Dover, a voice like a chain saw, cold, granite-colored eyes that missed nothing, hair like the English Channel on a gray choppy day, and a Scottish accent as frigid as chopped ice.

In a way, Mark thought, it was a shame that she had just missed Miss Hooting; the two of them might have hit it off.

Tea, with three kinds of scones, two kinds of shortbread, and cubes of frozen Glensporran in her Earl Grey, was just beginning to soothe Cousin Elspeth's ruffled feelings when there came a peal at the front doorbell.

"Inconseederate!" Cousin Elspeth sniffed again.

The caller proved to be Mr. Glibchick, the senior partner in the legal firm of Wright, Wright, Wright, Wright, and Wrong, who had their offices on the village green. All the Wrights and the Wrongs had long passed away, and Mr. Glibchick ran the firm with the help of his junior partner, Mr. Wrangle.

"What was it, dear?" inquired Mrs. Armitage when her husband returned, looking rather astonished, from his conversation with the lawyer.

"Just imagine—Miss Hooting has left us something in her will!"

Cousin Elspeth was all ears at once. Making and remaking her own will had been her favorite hobby for years past; and since arriving at the Armitage house she had already mentally subtracted four hundred pounds and a writing desk from Mark's legacy because he had neglected to pass her the jam, and was deliberating at present about whether to bequeath a favorite brown mohair stole to Harriet, who had politely inquired after her lumbago.

"Left us a legacy? What—in the name of goodness?" exclaimed

29

Mrs. Armitage. "I thought the poor old thing hadn't two pennies to rub together."

"Not money. Two mechanical helots, was what Mr. Glibchick said."

"Helots? What are they?"

"Helots were a kind of slave."

"Fancy Miss Hooting keeping slaves!" Harriet looked horrified. "I bet she beat them with her umbrella and made them live on burned toast-crusts."

"Little gels should be seen and not hairrd," remarked Cousin Elspeth, giving Harriet a disapproving glance, and changing her mind about the brown mohair stole.

Next day the mechanical slaves were delivered by Ernie Perrow in his tractor-trailer.

They proved to be two figures, approximately human in shape, one rather larger than life-size, one rather smaller, constructed out of thin metal piping, with plastic boxes for their chests containing a lot of electronic gadgetry. Their feet were large, round, and heavy; they had long, multi-hinged arms ending in prehensile hands with hooks on the fingers. They had eyes made of electric light bulbs and rather vacant expressions. Their names were stenciled on their feet: *Tinthea* and *Nickelas*.

"What gruesome objects!" exclaimed Mrs. Armitage. "For mercy's sake, let's give them to the next jumble sale; the very sight of them is enough to give me one of my migraines!"

Cousin Elspeth entirely agreed. "Whit seengularly reepulsive airrticles!"

But Mark and his father, seeing eye to eye for once, were most anxious to get the mechanical slaves, if possible, into working order.

"Besides, it would be most tactless to give them to a sale. Miss Hooting's friends would be sure to get to know."

"The things are in a horrible condition," pronounced Mark,

30

after some study of the helots. "All damp and dirty and rusty; the old girl must have kept them in some dismal outhouse and never oiled them."

"What makes them go?" inquired Harriet, peering at a damp, tattered little booklet, entitled Component Identification, which hung on a chain round Tinthea's neck.

"It seems to be lunar energy," said her father. "Which is pretty dicey, if you ask me. I never heard of anything running on lunar energy before. But that seems to be the purpose of those glass plates on the tops of their heads."

"More to 'em than meets the eye," agreed Mark, wagging his own head.

As it happened, the month of October was very fine. Hot, sunny days were succeeded by blazing moonlit nights. Tinthea and Nickelas were put out in the greenhouse to warm up and dry off. Meanwhile Mark and his father, each guided by a booklet, spent devoted hours cleaning, drying, oiling, and de-rusting the family's new possessions.

" 'Clean glazed areas with water and ammonia solution,' it says."

" 'Brush cassette placement with household detergent.' "

"Which is the cassette placement?"

"I think it must be that drawer affair in the chest."

"Chest of drawers," giggled Harriet.

Tinthea, which Mark was working on, let out something that sounded like a snort.

" 'Keep latched prehensile work/monitor selector function aligners well lubricated with sunflower or cottonseed oil.' Which do you think those are?"

"Its hands?" suggested Harriet.

Mr. Armitage, doing his best to clean the feet of Nickelas, which were in a shocking state, matted with dirt and old, encrusted furniture polish, accidentally touched a concealed lever

31

in the heel, and Nickelas began to hop about, in a slow, ungainly, but frantic way, like a toad in a bed of thistles. The helot's hand, convulsively opening and shutting, grasped the handle of Mr. Armitage's metal toolbox, picked up the box, and swung it at its owner's head. Mr. Armitage just managed to save himself from a cracked skull by falling over sideways into a tray of flowerpots. Nickelas then clumsily but effectively smashed eight greenhouse panes with the end of the toolbox, using it like a sledgehammer, before Mark, ducking low, managed to grab the helot's leg and flick down the switch.

"Oh, I see, *that*'s how they work!" Harriet pressed Tinthea's switch.

"Don't, idiot!" shouted Mark, but it was too late. Tinthea picked up a bucket of dirty, soapy water and dashed it in Harriet's face just before Mr. Armitage, with great presence of mind, hooked the helot's feet from under her with the end of a rake. Tinthea fell flat, and Mark was able to switch her off.

"I must say," said Mr. Armitage, suddenly becoming enthusiastic, "if we could get Nickelas, for instance, to take over all the digging and lawn mowing, and carry the trash can to the street, I should be quite grateful to old Miss Hooting for her legacy, and I'm sorry I ever called her a troublemaking old so-and-so."

"And maybe we can program Tinthea to wash dishes and make beds?" Harriet suggested hopefully.

But there was a long way to go before the helots could be set to perform any useful task with the slightest certainty that it would be carried out properly.

Tinthea, programmed to make the beds, showered sunflower oil liberally all over the blankets, and then tore up the sheets into shreds; she finished by scooping handfuls of foam rubber out of the mattresses, and unstringing all the bedsprings. The only bed spared was that of Cousin Elspeth, who always kept her bedroom door locked. Tinthea was unable to get into her room, though she returned to rattle vainly at the door handle all day long.

Nickelas, meanwhile, ran amok with the lawn mower, trundling it back and forth across the garden, laying flat all Mrs. Armitage's begonias and dahlias in fifteen minutes; Mark was able to lasso him and switch him off just before he began on the sweet peas.

"If I were ye, I'd smesh 'em with a hetchit," snapped Cousin Elspeth.

"I don't think *that* would be advisable. A witch's legacy, you know, should be treated with caution."

"A witch! Hech!"

Mr. Armitage telephoned the local museum to ask if they would accept the helots; but Mr. Muskin, the curator, was away for a month in Tasmania, collecting ethnological curiosities. The nearest National Trust mansion had to refer the possibility of being given two lunar-powered helots to its Acquisition Board; and the librarian at the village library was quite certain she didn't want them; nor did the Primary School.

For the time, Tinthea and Nickelas were locked in the cellar. "They won't pick up much lunar power there," said Mr. Armitage. They could be heard thumping gloomily about from time to time.

"I think they must have learned how to switch each other on," said Mark.

"It's a bit spooky having them down there," shivered Harriet. "I wish Mr. Muskin would come back from Tasmania and decide to have them."

Meanwhile, to everybody's amazement, a most remarkable change was taking place in Cousin Elspeth. This was so noticeable, and so wholly unexpected, that it even distracted the family's attention from the uncertainty of having two somewhat unbiddable helots in the cellar.

In fact, as Mr. Armitage said to his wife, it was almost impossible to believe the evidence of one's own eyes.

In the course of three weeks Cousin Elspeth's looks and her temper improved daily and visibly. Her cheeks grew pink, her eyes blue, and her face no longer looked like a craggy mountain landscape, but became simply handsome and distinguished. She was heard to laugh, several times, and told Mrs. Armitage that it didn't matter if the tea wasn't always Earl Grey; she remembered a limerick she had heard in her youth about the Old Man of Hoy, restored the writing desk to Mark in her will, and began to leave her bedroom door unlocked.

Curiously enough, after a week or two, it was Mrs. Armitage who began to think rather wistfully of the wasted helot manpower down there in the cellar lying idle. She told Mark to fetch Tinthea to help with the job of washing blankets, which Cousin Elspeth pointed out should be done before the winter.

"After all, as we've got the creatures we might as well make *some* use of them. Just carrying blankets to and fro, Tinthea can't get up to much mischief. But don't bring Nickelas, I can't stand his big staring eyes."

So Mark, assisted by Harriet, fetched the smaller helot from the cellar. They were careful not to switch her on until she was in the utility room, and the cellar door locked again on the inert Nickelas.

But Harriet did afterward recall that Tinthea's bulbous, sightless eyes seemed to watch the process of locking and unlocking very attentively.

For once, however, the smaller helot appeared to be in a cooperative mood, and she hoisted wet blankets out of the washing machine and trundled off with them into the garden, where

34

she hung them on the line without doing anything unpro-
grammed or uncalled-for, returning three or four times for a new
load. It was bright, blowy autumn weather, the leaves were
whirling off the trees, and the blankets dried so quickly that they
were ready to put back on the beds after a couple of hours.

"Ech! Bless my soul!" sighed Cousin Elspeth at tea, which was,
again, taken in the garden as the weather was so fine. "This
veesit has passed so quickly, it's harrd to realize that it will be
November on Thurrsday. I must be thinking of reeturrning to
my ain wee naist."

"Oh, but you mustn't think of leaving before our Halloween
party," said Mrs. Armitage quickly. "We have *so* much enjoyed
having you, Cousin Elspeth, you must make this visit an annual
event. It has been a real pleasure."

"Indeed it has! I've taken a grand fancy to your young folk."
Cousin Elspeth beamed benevolently on Mark and Harriet, who
were lying on their stomachs on the grass, doing homework
between bites of bread and jam.

"Where's Tinthea?" Harriet suddenly said to Mark. "Did you
put her away?"

"No, I didn't. Did you?"

Harriet shook her head.

Quietly she and Mark rose, left the group around the garden
table, and went indoors.

"I can hear something upstairs," said Mark.

A thumping could be heard from the direction of Cousin
Elspeth's room.

Harriet armed herself with a broom, Mark picked a walking
stick from the front-door stand, and they hurried up the stairs.

As they entered Cousin Elspeth's room, Tinthea could be seen
apparently admiring herself in the large looking glass. Then,
advancing to it with outstretched monitor selection function
aligners, she was plainly about to remove it from the wall when

35

Mark, stepping forward, tapped down her main switch with the ferrule of the walking stick. Tinthea let out what sounded like a cry of rage and spun half around before she lost her power and became inert, with dangling mandibles and vacant receiving panel; but even so it seemed to Harriet that there was a very malevolent expression in her sixty-watt eyes.

"What was *really* queer, though," Harriet said to her brother, "was that just before you hooked down her switch I caught sight of her reflection in the glass, and she looked—well, not like a helot, more like a person. There *is* something pecular about that mirror."

She studied herself in the glass.

"The first time I saw myself in it I thought I looked horrible. But now I look better."

Mark eyed his reflection and said, "Perhaps that's what's been happening to Cousin Elspeth; seeing herself in the glass day after day. . . ."

"Of *course*! Aren't you clever! So that's why old Miss Hooting wanted it! But what shall we do about Tinthea?"

"Put her back in the cellar. You take her legs. Don't touch the switch." Tinthea sagged heavily between them as they carried her back to the cellar. And when she was set down next to Nickelas, it seemed to Harriet that a wordless message flashed between the two bulbous pairs of sightless eyes.

The Armitages' Halloween party was always a great success.

This year Mrs. Armitage, with Cousin Elspeth and Harriet helping, produced a magnificent feast, including several Scottish delicacies such as haggis and Aberdeen Bun; Mark and Harriet organized apple-bobbing, table-turning, and fortune-telling with tea leaves (large Earl Grey ones), flour, lighted candles, and soot. The guests came dressed as trolls, kelpies, banshees, werewolves, or boggarts, and the sensation of the evening was the pair of helots, Tinthea and Nickelas, who, carefully and lengthily programmed by Mr. Armitage, who had been at it for days, passed around trays of cheese tarts, chestnut crunch fancies, and tiny curried sausages.

"But they're not real, are they?" cried Mrs. Pontwell, the vicar's wife. "I mean—they are Mark and Harriet, cleverly dressed up, aren't they, really?"

When she discovered that the helots were *not* Mark and Harriet she gave a slight scream and kept well out of their way for the rest of the evening.

Many of the guests remained, playing charades, until nearly midnight, but Cousin Elspeth, who intended to leave the following morning, retired to bed at half past ten.

"Och! I've just had a grand time," she said. "I never thocht I'd enjoy a party so well. But old bones, ye ken, need plainty of rest; I'll e'en take maself off to ma wee bed, for I must be up bricht and airrly the morn."

Her absence did not diminish the gaiety of the party, and Mrs. Armitage was serving cups of hot chocolate with rum in it while everybody sang Widecombe Fair, when piercing shrieks were heard from upstairs. Simultaneously all the lights went out.

"Och, maircy! Mairder! Mairder! Mairder!"

"Sounds as if someone's strangling Cousin Elspeth," said Mark, starting for stairs.

"Where did you put the matches?" said Harriet.

There were plenty of candles and matches lying around, but in the confusion, with guests and members of the family bumping about in the dark, it was some time before a rescue party, consisting of Mark, Mr. Armitage, and Mr. Shepherd from next door, were able to mount the stairs with candles and make their way to Cousin Elspeth's room.

They found that lady sitting up in bed in shawl and nightcap, almost paralytic with indignation.

37

"A deedy lot you are, upon my worrd! I could have been torrn leemb fra leemb before ye lifted a feenger!"

"But what happened?" said Mr. Armitage, looking around in perplexity.

"The mirror's gone!" said Mark.

"Whit happened? Whit *happened*? You unco' misshapen stravaiging shilpit monsters of your cam' glomping intil ma room—bauld as brass!—removed the meerror fra the wall, and glomped off oot again, as calm as Plato! Wheer they have taken it, I dinna speer—nor do I care—but thankful I am this is the last nicht in like I'll pass under *this* roof, and I'll ne'er come back afore death bears me awa', and it's only a wonder I didna die on the spot wi' petrification!" And Cousin Elspeth succumbed to a fit of violent hysterics, needing to be ministered to with burned feathers, sal volatile, brandy, snuff, hot-water bottles, and antiphlogistic poultices.

While this was happening, Mark said to Harriet, "Where do you suppose the helots have taken the mirror?"

"Back to the cellar? How did they get out?"

By this time most of the guests had gone. The blown fuse had been mended and the lights restored. Mark and Harriet went down, a little cautiously, to inspect the cellar, but found it empty; the lock had been neatly picked from inside.

As they returned to the hall, the telephone rang. Mark picked up the receiver and heard the vicar's voice.

"Mark, is that you, my boy? I'm afraid those two mechanical monsters of yours are up to something very fishy in the church-yard. I can see them from my study window in the moonlight. Will you ask your father to come along, and tell him I've phoned Officer Loiter."

"Oh, *now* what?" groaned Mr. Armitage on receiving this news, but he accompanied his children to the churchyard, which was only a five-minute run along the village street, leaving Mrs. Armitage in charge of the stricken Cousin Elspeth.

A large bright hunter's moon was sailing overhead, and by its light it was easy to see Nickelas and Tinthea hoisting up Miss Hooting's glass coffin. They had excavated the grave with amazing speed, and now carefully placed the coffin on the grass to one side of it. Then they laid the mirror, reflecting surface down, on top of the coffin.

As the Armitages arrived at one gate, the vicar and Officer Loiter came from the vicarage garden.

"Here! What's going on!" shouted Mr. Loiter, outraged. "Just you stop that—whatever you're doing! If you ask me," he added in an undertone to Mr. Pontwell, "that's what comes of burying these here wit— these old fairy ladies in churchyards along with decent folk."

"Oh dear me," said the vicar, "but we must be broadminded, you know, and Miss Hooting had been such a long-established member of our community—"

At this moment Nickelas and Tinthea, taking no notice of Mr. Loiter's shouts, raised the mirror high above the coffin, holding it like a canopy.

"What's the idea, d'you suppose?" Mark muttered to Harriet.

"So as to get the reflection of Miss Hooting inside the coffin—"

"Ugh!"

The coffin suddenly exploded with the kind of noise that a gas oven makes when somebody has been too slow in lighting the match. The helots fell backward, letting go of the mirror, which fell and smashed.

A large owl was seen to fly away from where the coffin had been.

Officer Loiter, very reluctantly, but encouraged by the presence of Mr. Pontwell and Mr. Armitage on either side, went forward

39

and inspected the coffin. But there was nothing in it except a great deal of broken glass. Nor was the body of Miss Hooting ever seen again.

"*I* think it was a plan that went wrong," said Harriet to Mark. "*I* think she hoped, if she had the mirror, it would make her young and handsome and stop her from dying."

"So she sent the helots to get it? Maybe," said Mark.

"What a shame the mirror got smashed. Because look at Cousin Elspeth!"

Cousin Elspeth, overnight, had gone back to exactly what she had been at the beginning of the visit—sour, dour, hard-featured, and extremely bad-tempered.

"Ye might have provided a drap of Earl Grey for my last breakfast!" she snapped. "And, as for that disgreeceful occurrence last nicht—aweel, the less said the better!" After which she went on to say a great deal more about it, and, as she left, announced that Mark would certainly not get the writing desk nor Harriet the mohair stole, since they were undoubtedly responsible for the goings-on in the night.

"Somehow I don't see Cousin Elspeth putting us through art school," mused Harriet, as the taxi rolled away with their cousin along the village street.

"That's a long way off," said Mark peacefully.

Mr. Armitage was on the telephone to Dowbridges, the auctioneers.

"I want you to come and fetch two robots and enter them in your Friday sale. Please send a truck at once; I'd like them out of the house by noon. Yes, *robots*; two lunar-powered robots, in full working order, complete with instruction booklets. Handy for workshop, kitchen, or garden; a really useful pair; you can price the large one at ninety pounds and the small at fifty."

On Friday Mrs. Armitage and Harriet attended the sale, and

returned to report with high satisfaction that both helots had been sold to old Admiral Lycanthrop.

"*He'll* give them what-for, I bet," said Mark. "*He* won't stand any nonsense from them."

But, alas, it turned out that the admiral, who was rather hard of hearing, thought he was bidding for two rowboats, and when he discovered that his purchase consisted instead of two lunar-powered mechanical slaves with awkward dispositions, he returned them, demanding his money back.

The Armitages came down to breakfast on Saturday to find Nickelas and Tinthea standing mute, dogged, and expectant, outside the back door. . . .

Black Dog

BY JOAN PHIPSON

"POPPY!"

Poppy looked around just in time to see her young brother disappear head first into a straggling and overgrown clump of rosebushes. Then a scream told her he was being prickled. She ran across the garden to pull him out.

"Keep still," she shouted as she caught hold of a waving foot. "You'll only get prickled more."

When she had got him out and he stood, tearful and red-faced in front of her, she said, "What happened? What made you fall into it?" The garden was certainly neglected and full of rioting plants that should have been cut back years ago, but the grass had been cut, and where Digby had been standing it was perfectly flat.

Digby rubbed the back of his forearm across his nose and said, "A big dog pushed me."

"What?"

"A big dog pushed me. A big black dog." His tears had stopped, and he looked at her now a little aggressively.

42

"Don't be silly, Dig. You know there's no dog here."

"There was. There was," Digby suddenly shouted at her. "It came and it gave me a push so I fell in the roses." His face was getting, if possible, redder than before.

"Well, where is it now?" Digby kept his eyes fixed on her face as she turned slowly, looking all around her.

"Maybe it went to the trash heap. I don't *know*." There was a frantic note in the last shouted word.

Poppy caught the note and put her arm around him. "Never mind. It's probably gone." After a moment's thought she said, "What were you doing, anyway? Where were you going?"

He pointed. "Only through the bushes to that big tree—to see what's behind it."

"There's nothing there. Only the trash heap. Anyway Dad said to keep away from it till he's had time to see there's nothing dangerous there."

"What dangerous?"

Poppy shrugged. "Oh, I don't know. Snakes and things, I suppose. Come on. Let's go in."

They had only been a week in the new house in Sydney and were not sure if they were going to like it. The best thing about it was that it was so near the park. Their mother had said that as the busy intersection leading to the park was so well controlled and signposted, they could go there on their own if they promised to be very careful. The house itself was old and as neglected as the garden. But even Poppy knew that poisonous snakes were unlikely to be found in the middle of the city.

"We can't imagine why it's been empty for so many months," their father had said. "But it's cheap enough for us, and it's handy to the university.

Their parents were both lecturers at Sydney University, which was why, Poppy often thought sadly, they had such terrible names. What sort of a name was Poppaea, for heaven's sake?

43

The second Sunday in the new house was wet, and for once they didn't mind because their mother had promised to unlock the doors of the two back rooms. These were apparently an addition to the house, made by the previous occupants. Some day their mother would get around to dealing with them. In the meantime they contained what their parents called junk and could well turn out to be articles of great price and value. They each went into a different room, and Poppy was busy looking through piles of old magazines and children's books when she heard Digby call. She found him kneeling on the floor in an attitude of prayer with an open exercise book in front of him.

"Here, Poppy," he said when her presence in the doorway blocked the only light there was. "See if you can read this. I can, but it's too slow."

She squatted down beside him. The exercise book was full of a small, squiggly writing and was divided into sections—Monday, Tuesday, Wednesday. "It's a diary," she said.

"I know. But look at the beginning." Digby reached across her arm and flipped the pages back. MADELEINE ROBINSON —HER BOOK. And it gave a date.

"This is only two years old," said Poppy. "It must be the girl who lived here last."

"Read it," said Digby. "Go on."

Poppy read—slowly at first, but gradually getting faster as she became used to the squiggly handwriting.

I have decided to start this diary because today is my thirteenth birthday and because it is the greatest birthday I have ever had. It is the greatest because of my birthday present. I never really thought Mom and Daddy would let me have a dog. I'd even given up asking for one. And now—here he is. My darling Bouncer. That's what I shall call him—Bouncer.

44

"What a silly name," said Digby.

I did really want a little puppy so he would grow up being mine. But Bouncer is so lovely and Daddy says the people he was bought from say he's quite young. In fact he has a pedigree. Imagine! And his birthday is on it. He's only a bit over a year old. The pedigree says he's a black Labrador. I thought they only came cream, or that biscuity color, but Bouncer's black and I love it. And I think he loves me already. Daddy's told me what words to use when I give him orders, like 'sit' and 'heel', and he does it immediately.

"She's underlined that," said Poppy.

Daddy says he's more obedient than I am. Daddy is funny. I'm allowed to take him walks on the lead and we can go to the park if we're careful of the crossing. Daddy says it's funny they wanted to get rid of such a lovely dog, especially as they're going to buy another. He asked them why and they said he was too big. But their next one is going to be a setter. I don't believe they told Daddy the truth. I don't care. I'm so happy Bouncer's mine now.

That was all for that day, and Poppy read on. Two days later Madeleine had taken Bouncer to the park. It seemed to have been a happy outing with Bouncer doing everything he should. Two or three uneventful days passed and Digby began to get restless. Then came an entry that was slightly more interesting.

It is sad, but I have to put in my diary that today Bouncer was NOT GOOD. I shan't tell Mom and Daddy because I want them to go on thinking Bouncer is perfect. But I'll tell you, diary. We were walking along the footpath quite ordinary and

45

peaceful when Bouncer suddenly pulled back. I told him to come on but he wouldn't. I pulled and scolded and it was all no good. After a while he just sat down. He looked quite sad, but he sat down just the same. I don't think we'd ever have got to the park if I hadn't led him back a bit and then crossed the road. He didn't seem to mind walking on the other side at all. And afterwards we had a lovely time in the park. Oh, it is nice having a dog. Perhaps if I had brothers and sisters I wouldn't love him so much. But now I'm glad I haven't any.

"I'd like a dog instead of you," said Digby.

"Just for that I won't read you any more," said Poppy.

But the next day Poppy had forgotten her threat, and, anyway, she was curious to know more about Madeleine and her dog.

Bouncer and I went to the park today.

"Doesn't she ever go to school?" said Digby.

I thought he might have been naughty again, but he wasn't. He came with me nicely all the way. But a funny thing happened. Just at the place where he had been naughty before and I was wondering if he would again, a boy on a scooter came whizzing past and bumped into me. I nearly fell over, but didn't quite. But I've got a bruise on my leg where the wheel hit me. Bouncer started to growl at him and I had to pull him away. Oh, I do love Bouncer. We got over that crossing without any trouble and had a lovely time in the park. We went to the lake and Bouncer was dying to have a swim. So (this is a secret, diary) I looked all around and there was no one there, so I let him off the lead and threw a stick into the lake. He plunged in straight away and swam out and got it and brought it back to me. Oh, I do love Bouncer. Then he shook himself all over me but I didn't mind and it soon dried and Mom never knew. I don't care, but I'm going to let him off again. Imagine bringing that stick all the way back!

"Shall I stop?" said Poppy.

"No," said Digby. "just go quickly over the boring bits." The next non-boring bit came about a week later.

I thought Bouncer had got over his naughty bits of disobedience but he did it again today. I am so cross with him. We were walking where we often go in the park, along a nice little path under some trees. Halfway along it Bouncer pulled back again. I scolded him like anything, and even smacked him, but he only shut his eyes and crouched down by my feet and when I pulled, dug his toes in. In the end I had to take him another way. Perhaps he is a moody dog and I didn't realize it. I shall try to handle him differently. But how? I couldn't bring myself to smack him hard. I might try tempting him with a bit of biscuit. I must remember to carry some in my pocket.

"I think she's silly," said Digby. "Let's stop now."

"No. Wait a bit," said Poppy, who had been reading ahead. "Listen to this. It's the next day."

I'd remembered to bring the biscuits, so we went along the same path under the trees and I thought if he stopped again I'd try to make him come with the biscuits. But this time he was a very good dog and seemed quite to have forgotten about yesterday. We were lucky, though. He'd just pulled me a bit off the path to smell something in the grass when there was a cracking noise over our heads and suddenly a branch came crashing down. The leaves and little branches fell all round us and I did have a scratch on my cheek, but the heavy part of the branch didn't

47

quite reach where we were. I've told Mom it was running past some bushes scratched my cheek. I don't want her to think there's anything to worry about in the park. All the same, it was funny.

That evening Poppy said to her mother, "Who were the people who had this house before us?" Digby stopped eating his dinner to wait for the answer. Ordinarily it was quite difficult to make Digby stop eating.

"Do you know, Arthur?" said their mother. "I never heard. I don't remember any mention of the previous owners."

Their father put down his knife and fork. "I did ask, but they were very vague. I got the feeling it was some time since the house had been occupied and the people had left in a hurry."

"Funny, when you come to think of it," said their mother.

"Perhaps I should have inquired. Why do you want to know, Poppy?"

"Just wondered," said Poppy. "Nothing, really." Suddenly she was sorry she had asked. They had not so far mentioned the diary, and now neither of them wanted to do so. Not until they had finished it.

It was on a Friday that Bouncer disobeyed for the third time.

Sometimes I think I don't understand Bouncer at all. Today was a lovely day—warm and sunny—and I had this lovely idea Bouncer and I would go to the park terribly early so there wouldn't be anyone about and I could let him chase sticks in the lake. I had biscuits in my pocket too, just in case. Mom and Daddy were quite pleased I'd thought of going so early. They said it was the nicest time of the day and I was sensible. I felt a bit deceitful, but I was doing it for Bouncer, wasn't I? Oh, you disappointing dog. There weren't many people about and we got to the park quite quickly. I didn't see anyone in the park at all—

*just a man jogging a long way away. And the lake was lying
there all still and shining with just a few birds flying about
chasing insects. I'd picked up some good sticks on the way so I
was all ready to give Bouncer a lovely time. But the silly dog
wouldn't go anywhere near the lake. He wouldn't even go across
the little wooden bridge. I took out my biscuits and gave him one
and he ate it like anything, but when I walked on to the bridge
and stood in the middle and held out another he wouldn't come.
I had the lead right at the end, pulling. But suddenly he jerked his
head back and the lead slipped out of my fingers.*

"I wonder she bothered," said Poppy.

"I bet I'd have bashed him with the sticks if he was mine,"
said Digby. "Go on, Poppy."

"Thought you liked Bouncer," said Poppy.

"All of a sudden I'm not so keen on him," said Digby. "But
go on."

*I had to go back over the bridge and catch him. He let me, but
he still wouldn't come over with me. In the end we never went
to the lake at all. Mom was surprised we got home again so early
and asked what was wrong. How did she know there was anything wrong?*

"I bet she had a long face," said Poppy. "That's all there is
for that day. But, look, there's a lot for the next day."

Digby looked over her shoulder. "Go on, then. Something
must have happened. Maybe silly old Bouncer got run over."

*It's quite late, and I'm a bit tired after all that's happened, but I
must write it down before I go to sleep. I think it might be important that I remember it. I think I might have to tell Mom and*

49

Daddy, but I'll wait till morning to decide. I don't know what to think, really. I thought I'd try Bouncer at the lake again because it would be such a pity if he could never swim again when he loves it so. We went again early in the morning, and it was a lovely day like yesterday. I was looking carefully at Bouncer in case he turned funny again, but this morning he really was bouncing and he came wherever I went and didn't seem to be worrying about anything. I could have gone to the lake the other way round, but I thought I'd try the bridge again, just to see. This time he galloped over in front of me and ran round the edge of the lake where the reeds are. The last thing I saw, really, was Bouncer chasing a seagull. Then, before I had time to get out of the way, a jogger came up from the path below the bridge and turned on to it. Perhaps he was watching Bouncer chasing the seagull too. I'm sure he never saw me, and I didn't see him until it was too late. He bumped into me, and splosh! There I was in the water. I didn't expect it to be so cold and all I thought as I went down was how soggy the cookies in my pocket would be. I fell in among the reeds and the water was muddy and rather smelly deeper down. I can swim all right, but it's more difficult with clothes and shoes on.

The trouble was those reeds. They got all tangled in my feet and I couldn't kick them away. I thought I'd burst before I came to the surface and was just beginning to wonder how long I could hold out when something bumped against me, and there was Bouncer, and I felt his teeth round my arm. His legs were scrabbling away in the water beside me and there are still scratches on my leg, as well as the tooth marks on my arm. But between us we got my feet free and up I popped. The jogger was just about to jump in too, but when he saw us he waded in at the edge and grabbed my other arm. Bouncer and I came out together, all wet and muddy and stinking. I was just going to thank the man when I heard Bouncer growling. The man sud-

*denly looked frightened and stepped back. I patted Bouncer and
told him not to be silly because the man had saved us. When he
began to wag his tail again I could see the man began to feel
better. He said to me, "Actually, it was that dog of yours saved
you. It was me that pushed you in. I'm dreadfully sorry. And
now I'm going to take you home and tell your parents how
sorry I am." It was nice of him really, because he couldn't have
expected Mom and Daddy to be very pleased. Anyhow, he insisted we come home in his car. I was glad because I looked
terrible and I didn't really want to walk along the public street
dripping and stinking.*

"Urk!" said Digby. "But go on, Poppy. It's getting exciting."

*Of course Mom and Daddy had to thank him for bringing us
home and they even asked him in for a cup of coffee, but he
said he'd be late for work and sort of backed out of the gate
apologizing all the time. He was a nice man and it wasn't his
fault. Daddy had to rush off too and Mom was left with Bouncer
and me to get clean. She tied poor Bouncer up at his kennel while
she got me into the bath and afterwards, when I was clean and
my dirty clothes in the wash, she hosed him, still tied up to his
kennel and she kept apologizing all the time, just like the jogger,
while she was doing it because, after all, it was Bouncer who got
me out of the reeds and the jogger had told them how wonderful
Bouncer was. Afterwards, when he was nice and clean again we
gave Bouncer a wonderful breakfast. Ordinarily he never has
breakfast, so it quite surprised him, but I'm afraid he is a bit
greedy, so he loved it. I was a bit late for school, and it took some
persuading for Mom to let me go. She seemed to think I ought
to stay in bed all day. But I was quite all right and it would have
been silly. So I left her to look after Bouncer and I caught the
bus.*

51

"See, she did go to school after all, Digby," said Poppy.

Digby was looking thoughtful. Then he said, "I'm sorry I didn't like Bouncer for a while there. He was really a good sort of a dog, wasn't he?"

"There's more," said Poppy, who had been reading ahead again. "Listen."

All day at school I kept thinking about it. I thought it was funny about Bouncer when the branch fell. Then I remembered about the scooter. And now here was the lake. Sometimes I would think it was all just chance that the things had turned out that way. Then I would think it couldn't be. Some of the day I was dying to get home so I could just look at Bouncer. I don't know why I thought I could tell by looking at him. The more I thought, the more I believed it couldn't have been just chance. And if it wasn't, what should I do about it? If I decided Bouncer behaved like that on purpose, how long should I go on avoiding the places where he did it? Forever? The more I thought, the more difficult it all seemed to be. I still didn't know when I got home again. I hadn't said anything up to dinnertime, and when Mom and Daddy and I were all sitting together and Bouncer, as a special treat, was sitting under the table, everything seemed so safe and ordinary I decided the best thing was just to forget it and not worry. I felt like that till I got into bed. Then I could feel it all creeping back into my mind. I began to wake up more and more. In the end I couldn't stand it another minute. I got out of bed and went into the sitting room. Mom and Daddy were sitting watching the television, when I said, "I've come to ask you something." They must have known it was serious because Daddy turned the television off at once and they got all ready to listen. So I told them about the three times he wouldn't come with me. I had to tell about him swimming in the lake but they never said anything. In the end it was Daddy who said it was just coincidence and I wasn't to take any notice. And Mom said sometimes things did happen like that just by chance and I wasn't to let it worry me. If Bouncer wouldn't come again I was to take him another way and forget about it. Daddy even wondered if it was this naughty habit of Bouncer's that made his last owners get rid of him. "They're sticklers for discipline," he said. So now I feel much better and I know I'll be able to sleep. But I did want to write it all down before.

Poppy stopped reading. "What do you think, Digby?"

"Her Dad was right, I reckon. If Bouncer knew, why didn't he stop it happening?"

"Perhaps he just didn't know enough," said Poppy. "I'd have been careful if I was Madeleine. Too spooky."

"Girls always think things are spooky."

"No more than boys. You're stupid and I won't read any more."

Digby reached for the book. "I'll read it myself, then."

Poppy snatched it away. "No you won't." She turned over the page. "Oh."

"What?" Digby leaned over.

"There's not much more."

"Go on, then. Read it. Poppy."

You'll never believe this, diary, but today Bouncer just wouldn't cross the intersection to the park. I tried to make him, and I even smacked him hard. But he wouldn't. I'll do what Daddy says and take no notice. Tomorrow I'm going to the park just the same.

"That's all," said Poppy. She closed the exercise book.

For a time they just sat looking at the book. Then Digby said in a whisper, "What do you think happened?"

Poppy shook her head. She picked up the book and riffled

through the leaves. "There's nothing else," she said. "Nothing else at all."

It was the next weekend that their father decided to clear out the trash heap. Trash heaps, like locked rooms, sometimes revealed unexpected treasures, and Poppy and Digby went to help. Their father was striding in among some big clumps of half-dead, straggling shrubs not far from the rosebush Digby had fallen into when he suddenly made an exclamation and they saw him jump back.

"A snake?" said Digby hopefully.

But it was not a snake. "Just stand back," said their father, "till I get this thing uncovered." This thing turned out to be a well that none of them had suspected. Their father put his foot through the rotting wooden well-cover. "We'll have to have that filled up," he said. "It's dangerous."

It was after they found the broken dog kennel underneath half an iron tank and an old refrigerator that Poppy said to Digby, "That was Bouncer's kennel. Digby, are you sure you saw a big black dog when you fell into the roses?"

Digby stood and looked at her and his eyes grew very round. Slowly he nodded his head. "I would have run right into the well," he whispered.

Two days later the man came with a truck to take the half tank and the refrigerator and all the other trash to the dump. He was just heaving up the dog kennel when they got back from school.

"Oh, stop," said Poppy.

"That's Bouncer's kennel," said Digby. "You can't take it."

"But it's all busted," said the man. "And where's the dog, anyway?"

It was lucky their mother was at home. She could see no sense in keeping such a piece of wreckage, but she could see no harm in it, either. And her children unaccountably sounded quite desperate.

When the man had gone, a little puzzled, and telling them to watch the crossing into the park because of the way kids kept getting bowled over, Digby said, "We might have lost Bouncer."

Poppy nodded. "If the kennel had gone, we might. And we need him. Come on, Digby. Let's go to the park."

Billy's Hand

~♦~

BY ADÈLE GERAS

I DON'T KNOW WHAT YOU'VE HEARD ABOUT BILLY'S HAND. Everyone in the class has been so busy inventing, embroidering, twisting and magnifying what really happened that it's difficult to sort out the truth. Julia thinks, for instance, that it was a sort of collective waking nightmare brought on by the cheese in our sandwiches: I ask you! So that's what I've decided to do: tell you exactly what happened, exactly as I remember it. And I do remember it—after all, wasn't it me that Billy called for in that horrible moment? Miss Peters was there too, of course, but she's not going to give you an account of the events of that day, you can bet your boots on that. "Hysteria," she was muttering in the ambulance afterward. "An illusion induced by hysteria." I don't know about that. I thought an illusion was something you saw that turned out to be not there at all, and you can't say that about Billy's hand, not really. But I'm jumping ahead. I mustn't do that. Back to the beginning.

Billy's hand. Doesn't it just sound like something from a horror movie? Could it be severed and dripping with blood? I'm sorry if this is a disappointment to anyone, but there are no severed heads, vampires, ghosts of the chain-rattling variety, headless horses or haunted graveyards in this story; no matter what Sharon and Tracy may have told you. What you're going to hear may be more or less terrifying, I don't know, but I can say quite truthfully that I'd rather meet a couple of thirsty vampires any day than go through that again, perhaps because vampires, etc., have become quite cozy now that we see them on T.V. such a lot.

There's another reason why I should be the one to tell the story and that's because I'm Billy's cousin. I'm not only his cousin but I live next door to him and have all my life. And there's something else: I'm probably the only person in the world, apart from his parents, who likes Billy. The truth is, he's awful. He's a bully, the worst sort of bully, nasty and thoughtful about his unkindness, as if he spends a great deal of time working out just the right torment for the person he's getting at. I know what they say about bullies, that they're all cowards at heart and that you only have to stick up for yourself and they'll run away. Well, our Billy's not like that. He's completely fearless. Or he was completely fearless, I should say. Before that school trip, there wasn't a person on earth he wouldn't have fought, and no one he would have feared to tease or terrify, not even kids with big brothers who threatened to have him beaten up after school, or those with dads who would report him to the Head as soon as look at him.

So why do I like him? Even love him a bit, perhaps. Well, firstly, as the vampires would say, blood is thicker than water. All my life he's been there like a big brother, and no amount of remembering the gouged-out eyes of my favorite dolls, or those dreadful frogs he used to put in my bed because they were my special terror, can change that. He could always run faster, climb higher, and shout louder than me, and so he gave me something to aim for, something to copy. Secondly, he became bored of bullying me by the time we were five. We went to school together (we've been in the same class all along) and there, spread out for his pleasure, were dozens and dozens of new victims, all fresh and ready with huge buckets of tears still waiting to be shed. I learned never to cry years ago. Thirdly, when we moved up into secondary school, he became a kind of protector, sheltering me from the lesser bullies of the class. "Don't touch Kim Harrison," they used to say, "or that Billy'll get you, good and solid. She's his cousin or something." And I was grateful for this protection, and did his homework for him most nights. I also made him promise to lay off all my best friends, but sometimes he forgot. He's not very bright, except at his bullying, you see, but at that he's fiendishly clever. One day, he cut off Shirley's thick, long plait of golden hair in the middle of a film we were watching in the school hall. It was a film about deserts, and suddenly Shirley shrieked and all the lights went on, and there was the cut-off plait under her chair, all lumpy and lifeless and horrid. I looked for Billy, but he was on the other side of the room. I'll never know how he moved so fast, nor what he did with the scissors. The Head never found out who had done it. There was no proof, though I bet he had his suspicions. Shirley cried and cried for hours all through dinner, even though it was sausages, which were her very best food of all. I screamed at Billy all the way home:

"You monster! How could you do it? I *told* you to leave Shirley alone. How could you? I'm not doing your homework for you for a month. Maybe I'll never do it again."

"I forgot," Billy said, smiling. "That she was your friend, I mean. Doesn't matter, it'll grow. Teach her not to be so vain."

"How come you're the one to punish everyone for their faults? Who gave you the right to teach people lessons? Brute, beast, I hate you!"

Billy didn't seem to be listening. "If you don't do my home-work," he said, after some thought, "I'll clobber you so's you'll stay clobbered, know what I mean?" He winked at me.

"Clobber away, go ahead and see if I care, you bullying gas-bag!" I shouted and ran ahead. I'd managed to become a bit fearless myself over the years, and at that moment I was so furious about Shirley's hair, I'd have taken on a whole army of Billys.

"Run away, go on!" he yelled after me. "Run away! GIRL! That's all you are, a silly girl. You only care about stupid Shirley's stupid old hair. You don't care about me."

It wasn't until much later, in bed, that I began to wonder if Billy was jealous of Shirley. I hadn't been playing with him nearly so much lately. It was very peculiar.

Anyway, one day we went on a class outing to the Castle, a kind of history outing it was supposed to be. We went in a bus with Miss Peters (we call her Miss Piggy because she's plump and pink, with yellow hair bouncing round her shoulders, and a really turned-up nose) and Mr. Melville, who's dry and long, like a stick with hair on top, and glasses. We took packed lunches from school and ate them in a field on the way. Most people were quite glad to be out for the afternoon, it didn't really matter what the reason was, but there were a few moaners, who kept saying things like:

"Boring old pile of rubbish."

"Should've skipped."

"Why can't they leave us here to play football and collect us on the way back?"

"Are there dungeons? I vote we lock Miss Piggy in with Old Melville!"

"I wouldn't mind so much, only they'll probably get us to write about it tomorrow. Do a project even."

We drove a bit more after lunch, and when we first saw the

Castle through the windows of the bus, everybody stopped talking. It was a very castle-like castle, square and high on top of a hill with tall, silent walls of thick, dark stone. I think Shirley was expecting a dainty turreted thing, like the Walt Disney cartoon castle in *Cinderella* or *The Sleeping Beauty.*

"Gosh," she said to Miss Piggy, "it's so square and grim-looking."

Miss Piggy smiled: "Well, dear, it *is* used as a prison still, you know."

"Will we see them?" Shirley was anxious. "The prisoners, I mean?"

"No, of course not. We shall be going on the guided tour, and they're in quite another part of the buildings."

"We might hear their screams," said Billy, and shrieked with laughter.

"William Harrison, behave yourself," said Old Melville, "or the screams you hear will be your own."

"What'll you do, sir, lock him in the dungeons?"

"Chain him to the wall?"

"Hang, draw and quarter him?"

"Stick his head on a spike on the castle walls?"

"SHUT UP!" I shouted, standing up in my seat. "Don't be disgusting!" I sat down again next to Shirley.

"I think boys are revolting sometimes," I said.

"It's not just the boys," said Shirley. "Lynn was the one who suggested chaining him to the wall."

"Then girls are revolting, too. Everyone's horrible to Billy."

"Billy's pretty horrible to them, though, isn't he?"

"Yes, I know. He is. Don't let's spoil the day by talking about him. I'm looking forward to it."

"I'm not, really." Shirley sighed. "All these old things, they just don't seem real to me. I can't sort of take them seriously, know what I mean? It's as if it was a made-up story or something.

I can't get worked up about things that happened donkey's years ago, not like you."

After what happened to Billy, I asked myself over and over again whether I hadn't imagined the whole thing, but that was only to try and comfort myself, to convince myself that everything was in my own mind and nowhere else. But that's nonsense. It happened to everyone. To Billy most of all, of course, but something, something strange and something that I can't explain happened even to Miss Piggy and Old Melville.

When we got out of the bus, we went up some stone steps and waited for a while outside a small, wooden door that looked as if it hadn't been opened for centuries. But it did open, quite silently on well-oiled hinges, and we went in.

The first room we saw was a courtroom, large and almost round, with high, light ceilings and a lot of heraldic shields up on the wall. The guide turned on a little silver tape recorder, and a voice spoke into the silence of us all sitting there, listening. The voice, floating up into the carvings over the windows, told us where to go next, and we followed the real guide into a small, round, high room with tall walls, like a tower. Another tape recorder (same voice) told us all about the things we could see all around us. Lots of us perked up a bit in this room, because it was full of horrible things in glass cases, like whips and cat-o-nine-tails and an iron, trap-like contraption called a scold's bridle, which was put over women's heads and was supposed to stop them talking too much.

"My mom could do with that," someone said.

"What are those, sir, those kind of chains on the walls?"

"Neck chains," said Mr. Melville. "Those big ones. And foot chains. Used to shackle people together on their way to the ships, to be deported to Australia."

Near the wall was a large wooden chair. Billy stood staring at it.

61

"What are you looking at that carefully for?" I said.

"I'm trying to see how it works. It's jolly clever. You strap someone in, you see, and the more they struggle, the tighter the straps get. They used it for lunatics."

"Charming, I'm sure," I said and tried to laugh but the laughter wouldn't come, Everybody had turned quite quiet, even though the place was the opposite of gloomy. It should have been spooky, but it wasn't. It was neat, and brightly lit and quite cheerful in a peculiar kind of way. Even the dungeons, with thick stone walls and no light at all when the wooden doors were closed, were not too bad. We all took turns having the guide shut us in for a moment, and it wasn't very creepy, not with four or five others giggling and joking beside you. Miss Piggy came in with us, and Mr. Melville went with the boys. Billy looked rather pale when he came out. He wasn't talking at all.

"I think it's a bit dull," Shirley said.

"No, it must have been awful," I replied, trying to picture it in detail and failing miserably. "Think of that dark and the cold all the time, for months or years!"

"I know," said Shirley. "I know it was awful. But I can't *feel* it." I said nothing because I couldn't really feel it either, and I was worried to think that my imagination was losing its power. It was like losing your sight, in a funny kind of way.

The next room we went into was also a courtroom, and the tape-recorded voice spoke hollowly of the trials that had taken place there. A kind of double metal bracelet was fixed to the wall of the prisoner's dock, and in the olden days, people found guilty had their hands locked into the iron bands and the letter M for "Malefactor" branded on the fleshy part of their hand below the thumb. The branding iron was still there, too. I didn't stay to look at it more carefully. Suddenly, I wanted to leave, quickly. Just for a split second, I thought I had seen him: the judge.

Dressed in purple, or red, or black, I couldn't quite see, and he was gone almost before my imagination had pictured him there, thin, skeleton-like under the carved oak canopy above him, with eyes that could burn you deep inside more thoroughly than that hideous branding iron in the dock. My imagination had come back with a vengeance, I thought as I hurried out. But Shirley had seen him, too. She was white.

"Did you see him?"

"Who?" (I was playing for time.)

"A man. Thin and white-faced, like a skull. He was only there for a second. Then he was gone."

"You must have imagined it." I wasn't ready to admit anything at that stage.

Shirley cheered up. "I'm sure I saw that man, but he can't have been real, can he, or he would have stayed put. Real people don't just vanish, do they?"

"No, of course they don't. Come on."

Shirley came, looking quite comforted. I couldn't think why. Surely she would rather have seen a real person who stayed put? Hadn't she worked out yet that if what she saw wasn't real, it must have been something else?

The next room we went into (the last room we saw, as things turned out) is just a blur in my memory. I can't remember a word of the tape recording, nothing about the room at all except —well. As soon as we were all crowded in, a shaft of sunlight came straight through the narrow window, and all of a sudden it was as if that beam of brightness was the only thing in the world. I looked and looked at it, feeling as if I was drowning in the light. While this was happening, I could feel without knowing why, that everyone else was drawn into the light, too, staring, staring and powerless to move. I vaguely remember Miss Piggy's mouth hanging open. The light faded a little, and then came the noise, so much noise that I covered my ears. There was mist now outside the window, mist everywhere, although the sun was still shining, I'm sure of that. Through the mist, I saw them. We all saw them. We talked about it afterward. There were thousands and thousands of them: faces, people, screaming throats and waving arms, all over the castle walls. It was hard to see what they were wearing, but it wasn't modern clothes. The people were watching for something, waiting for something. I knew I didn't want to see what it was they were waiting for. I took a deep breath and made a huge effort and turned my eyes away from the window. I saw Old Melville trembling, and blinking under his thick glasses. His mouth was opening and closing and his face was getting redder and redder. It was as if he were trying to speak and nothing would come.

"Are you all right, Mr. Melville?" I said, because I honestly thought he was about to have a heart attack or something, and then two things happened. Mr. Melville shrieked out: "For God's sake, close your eyes, oh, close them, close them now. Don't look at it! Don't look at that hideous, that hideous . . . gibbet. Oh, save these children, save them from seeing it!" He fell on his knees, crying like a first grader. Miss Piggy rushed toward him, and everyone turned to see what the commotion was about. I glanced at the window. Nothing. No people. Silence. No gallows. I was just breathing a sigh of relief when I heard Billy. Hadn't he been with us all the time?

"Kim! Kim! Kim!" The scream went right through me, into my bones. I felt so cold, I didn't know how I would move. But I ran. Faster than I've ever run before, shouting:

"Billy. Billy, I'm coming!" I could hear footsteps behind me, and Miss Piggy calling "Wait, Kim, wait for me!"

Billy was crouched on the floor of the courtroom, clutching his hand between his knees.

"My hand!" he moaned. "Oh, Kim, look at my hand. I can't stand it, the pain, how will I ever stand it?" He was crying and crying and rolling around to try and find a way to sit that wouldn't hurt so much.

"Let me see," I said. "Come on, Billy, let me see it."

"No, no," he sobbed, "nobody must see it. Please, Kim, don't look!"

"Don't be such an idiot," I said. "How can we get it better if I don't see it?"

I reached down and took Billy's hand. Under the thumb, on the fleshy part of his left hand, clear as clear, the letter M was branded into the flesh: red, sore, burning. I dropped his hand in terror and turned to run away and find help. I bumped straight into Miss Piggy.

"Billy's hand is branded!" I shrieked. "It is! It is!"

"Shush, child, quiet. Sit down. Let me look at it." She sat down on a bench, and put her coat round me and went to look at Billy.

"He's fainted," she said. Mr. Melville and the others had pushed their way into the room.

"Fetch an ambulance," said Miss Piggy.

"He's been branded," I cried. "Look at his hand."

"It's hurt, certainly," said Miss Piggy. "An ugly bruise and a bad cut, that's all, but it must be very painful. I wonder how he did that?"

"It's *not* a bruise," I shouted. "It's a mark. There's the branding iron. Touch it. Go on. Touch it." I wouldn't touch it. I wouldn't look at the judge's chair. I knew he would be there, the judge. Billy and I went in the ambulance with Miss Piggy. Mr. Melville took the others back to school.

Billy's hand has a scar on it now. Just a coincidence, I suppose, that the scar happens to have the shape of an M? That's the official story. They also said, the teachers and doctors, that the scar would fade. But it hasn't. Sometimes it's very pale and you can hardly see it, but sometimes it's very red and nasty. Billy rather enjoyed showing it off at first, but he never, not even to me, said a word about how he came to bear the mark in the first place.

Mr. Hornet and Nellie Maggs

◥◤

BY ALISON MORGAN

"NO, DENIS, I AM NOT ALWAYS PICKING ON YOU," SAID MR. Hornet, in his high, thin voice that seemed to come from the back of his nose. "It is just that I take you as I find you, and I find you. . . ." Mr. Hornet paused, lightly tapping a ruler on the grubby exercise book before him until he had the full attention of the class, ". . . repulsive."

The class tittered politely, and Mr. Hornet continued, rocking back on his heels, "Do you know what repulsive means, Denis?"

"Nope."

Mr. Hornet glanced around the waiting pack. "Can anyone kindly enlighten our Denis?"

A forest of hands shot up. They might not be too sure about "repulsive," but they knew Mr. Hornet, and they knew Denis. Each awaited the teacher's nod.

"Nasty, sir."

"Dirty."

67

"Untidy." This was felt to be a weak contribution, and the class gathered itself to do better.

"Turns you off, sir." Somebody in the opposite corner made a realistic vomiting noise. Now the hunt was on.

"Picks his nose."

"Stinks, sir."

"Tells lies."

Suddenly Emma was on her feet, from the row in front of Denis, three desks along. Her neck was flushed crimson under the mane of ginger hair, and she held her arm high as she stood very straight and still. Mr. Hornet could not ignore her. "Emma?"

"Sad, sir."

One or two children giggled at Emma for having missed the point of the game, and someone tried to bring her in line by saying, "Yeah, miserable as sin." But Emma stood there, spear-straight and fiery, while the joke fizzed about the classroom like a punctured balloon and dropped, a tattered shred, to the floor. Then she sat down.

In the silence that followed, Denis squinted sideways at her as he sat with head sunk low over grimy knuckles, but she never looked at him. If she had, he would have killed her or, worse, cried.

For some reason, he started thinking about Nellie Maggs.

Nellie lived in one of a pair of roadside cottages on the edge of town, out beyond the gas-works and the last filling station. Denis lived in the other one, with his half-brother, Mark, and Mark's wife and three-year-old daughter. There was another baby expected soon.

Nellie Maggs was going to be seventy next birthday. She had something wrong with her hips, that made her heave her body from side to side, like a duck, only she didn't move her legs fast like a duck, but slowly, as though each leg had to be thought about in turn before it would move. She had grayish-white hair, which she tucked in straggling wisps behind her big ears, and a wide, wide mouth. Her face was darker than her hair, and blotched, the color of a light-brown frog, and when her great grin broadened her face, that was exactly what she looked like, a kind, cheerful, ugly frog.

Denis could not remember his mother at all, because she had only stayed with his father for a couple of years, and then gone off. No wonder, people had said, for Denis's father, apart from being twice her age, was well known as the local drunk. When Denis was about eight, his father, weaving his way home from the pub, had stepped in front of a car pulling out from the filling station. There had been a funeral, and Mark had married Tracy, who came from a nice clean, respectable family. Mark had been careful during the years he had been courting her never to bring her back to the cottage while his disreputable old father was alive, but now she moved in and quickly turned the old place into a spotless copy of her parents' home. Only Denis remained as a shabby reminder of the old days.

For most of his childhood, when no one else was around to look after the little Denis, Nellie Maggs had done it. She used to sit him on her crippled knees and read him fairy stories.

Denis stirred in his school desk, remembering the occasion which, looking back, marked the end of the bright days of child-hood. It was when he was first conscious of being laughed at.

Nellie Maggs was reading him a story. " 'What, kiss an ugly old frog like you?' screamed the princess. And she threw the poor frog across the floor," read Nellie Maggs. Denis could still see the bright pictures and the pattern of print on the book that told the story of the princess who kisses the ugly frog to gain a wish, and turned the frog into a handsome prince.

"So now you know what you must do, my lovey, when you want something. Just you find the ugliest old frog you can, and give it a lovely big kiss."

69

Denis had stared up at the leathery brown cheek a few inches from his face, and then he had flung his arms round her neck and kissed her, just by the bristly wart on her chin.

He hadn't minded when she cackled with laughter; but he minded the way his father laughed, and Mark, and Tracy, as the story was passed around for their amusement. It had even caught up with him at school, years later.

Life from then on seemed to be full of mockery. His father mocked him for being frightened and running to Nellie Maggs when he was drunk; Mark mocked him for being stupid; later Tracy mocked him. "Denis, don't eat so disgusting." "Denis, wash your hands." "Didn't your father teach you nothing?" And at school it was all mockery.

Since Nellie Maggs was the only person who didn't seem to despise him, Denis could take a little comfort that she, at least, was a lower creature than he was. "That old witch,'" Mark called her, and Tracy was always afraid that germs would seep through from next door, but when Denis started calling her "that old witch" too, he got scolded for it. Once he tagged on to a gang of boys who threw stones through her windows and ran away. Emma, he thought, would not have done *that.* . . .

The end of afternoon school arrived, and Denis was just leaving the classroom when Mr. Hornet called him back. "You can wait, Denis, till the rest of the class has gone."

"Oh, thanks," muttered Denis, under his breath. The mean old devil. But then, old Hornet always had it in for him, just as the rest of his class had. Dregs, the other children called him. Not Denis the Menace, like other Denises. Just Dregs. When Mr. Hornet beckoned him to come up to the teacher's desk, he shambled slowly forward.

"I've got something for you," said Mr. Hornet. He was feeling down inside his breast pocket, and came out with a tiny box. It appeared to have been homemade out of cardboard, about the size of a sugar lump, and all bandaged up with sticky tape. It looked as if it had been in Mr. Hornet's pocket for a long time, for bits of fluff and dirt clung to it.

"In this box," said Mr. Hornet, "I have one happy day."

Denis stared at him blankly. Then little threads of thoughts, like worms, began to wriggle in from the fringes of his mind. Was Hornet going mad? Was *he* mad? Or had he not been listening properly, and Mr. Hornet had actually said something quite different? But the obvious things, like detention, didn't come in sticky boxes the size of a sugar lump. For the box was there, in Mr. Hornet's fingers, which were trembling as he tried to tear off the sticky tape.

"Scissors," said Mr. Hornet. "Or a knife. Oh, quick!" He sounded as cross as usual, and in a tearing hurry, but scared, too, as though he might not be able to go through with whatever he had decided to do.

Denis had neither, but he produced his old bent compasses, and Mr. Hornet managed to stab and wrench at the tape till he had slit one side open, jabbing his finger in the process so that the blood oozed out. Denis suddenly felt frightened at the thought that he was alone in the classroom with a madman armed with a pair of compasses. Ignoring that, Mr. Hornet shook something out into the palm of his hand and held it out for Denis to see.

It was a small roundish object, rather like a pearl, only a bright, glowing red, semi-transparent, so that one could see a pinprick of gold glimmering and flickering away right in the heart of it.

"There," said Mr. Hornet, "one happy day."

"Pardon?" said Denis.

"Now listen carefully," said Mr. Hornet, and for once Denis did. Surprise had blown his mind clear of all its usual layers of fluff, and he remembered every word that Mr. Hornet said for

71

the rest of his life. "When I put this jewel, or seed, into your hand, it will turn into two. One you swallow, and it will give you one perfectly happy day. The other one you must keep and give to someone else, just as I am giving you this one now, and just as somebody once gave one to me."

What a funny thing to give to Mr. Hornet, Denis thought. He must have been given it in the school holidays, because he's never had a happy day in school, to my certain knowledge. Bad-tempered, mean old creature, always.

"Why me?" he asked. Why, indeed, Mr. Hornet had never tried to disguise his contempt for Denis. Perhaps it was all a trick to poison him.

"Because you need it," said Mr. Hornet. "Now take it, quick, before I change my mind."

Denis thought there could not be any harm in just holding it in his hand. That way he could see if it really turned into two, like Mr. Hornet had said.

He held out his open hand and Mr. Hornet took the pearl-like thing between his finger and thumb and placed it carefully in Denis's grimy palm. At once it began to roll about, hither and thither, like a live thing, in the small cup of his hand, too fast for the eye to follow the movement; only the color danced in his hand, red and gold, bright as a flame, but without heat. Gradually the dancing colors slowed and settled, and in the palm of his hand lay two identical red-gold pearls.

Mr. Hornet gave a great sigh. The tenseness and irritability went out of him and he smiled. "Ah!" he said. Then he put a friendly hand on Denis's shoulder. "Run along now," he said, "as soon as you have swallowed one of them. Then you'll have your happy day tomorrow."

"Tomorrow's a school day," said Denis. How could he have a happy day at school?

Mr. Hornet was still unaccountably smiling. "Your happy day

will look after itself," he said, "but I don't suppose it will include school. If you just turn up again on Thursday, I shan't ask my questions about tomorrow."

Denis looked at the two little objects in his hand. "Why can't I swallow both, and have two happy days?" he said. One didn't seem much, out of a lifetime.

"You can," said Mr. Hornet. "But then that's the end of it. You see, it only doubles when you give it to someone else. The great mistake—I see it now—is hanging on to the second one too long. You must give it to someone else who needs it—don't wait, like I did, for years and years. Now, just swallow the one and keep the other safe."

"It's not poison, is it?" Mr. Hornet looked so friendly that Denis felt able to ask the question and trust the answer.

"No," said Mr. Hornet, "and it's not a drug, either. The things you'll do on your happy day will be real things, not just dreams."

"It sounds like magic," said Denis.

"Yes," said Mr. Hornet. "That's what it is. You get half the magic tomorrow, and the rest later."

Denis swallowed the pearl. It did not taste of anything in particular, nor did it make him feel any different. Mr. Hornet gave him the comic little box for the second pearl, and found some more sticky tape to fasten it with. "Don't lose it," he said. "Have a happy time tomorrow, and I'll see you in school on Thursday." And he trotted jauntily off down the school staircase, humming a tune.

Denis fell asleep that night dreaming of all the things he would like to do on his happy day. They included a car chase, a shoot-out in a sewer and another in a multi-story garage, foiling single-handed a plot to blow up the world, and being a boy-emperor on horseback, leading his army into battle.

He was wakened early by Mark coming in to say the baby was

73

about to arrive and he was taking Tracy into the hospital and dropping the three-year-old at her grandmother's. "I won't get back till late tonight," said Mark. "Here's some money for you to go to the pictures and get yourself something to eat."

As soon as they had gone, Denis dressed, had breakfast and went to the railway station. There was a poster saying "Take a rail trip to Biddleton-by Lea and visit the County Show." There were pictures of shire horses with arched necks and ribbons in their tails, motorcyclists flying through fiery hoops, vintage cars and a fairground.

Denis went to the ticket office. "Half return to Biddleton," he said.

"Two pounds exactly," said the clerk, and flicked out the ticket. "You're early. Hoping for a job there?"

"Yeah," said Denis.

"I've got an uncle, has a farm there. They're always desperately busy the morning of the Show, getting stock ready. I used to help there myself when I was a kid. Good fun it was, too. When you come out from the station, don't take the road into town. Turn left—it's about half a mile up the lane. Say Joe sent you."

"I will," said Denis. "Thanks."

If the red pearl made magic, it made very businesslike magic, Denis thought as he sat on the little train bustling out into the rich June countryside.

He found the farm without trouble. There was a magnificent shire horse, big as an elephant, tied up in the yard. A frisky colt was cavorting about on the end of a rope. "Steady, steady now," called the farmer, but the colt wasn't interested in being steady.

Seeing Denis hovering about in the yard, the farmer said "Looking for a job?"

"Yes, please. Joe sent me."

"Get up on that horse, then, and carry on braiding the mane from where I had to leave off. Not afraid of horses, are you?"

74

"No," said Denis. He had never thought about it, but the horse looked as steady as a rock. He climbed onto a wall, and so onto the horse's back. It was warm and solid. He studied the way the red ribbon interlaced the shining black mane, and set to work. His fingers had an unaccustomed nimbleness.

"Oh, bless you," said the farmer's wife, hurrying through the yard. "You're as welcome as the birds in spring. Black Diamond trusts you. You've got good hands with a horse, I can see that."

"You've made a tidy job of that," said the farmer, when he had done. "Now, can you polish up his coat till he shines like his name—Black Diamond?"

"I'll try," said Denis. When it was time to set off with him to the showground, everybody said what a god job Denis had done.

"You'll have to lead him around the ring," said the farmer. "After all the work you've put into him, I reckon we've got a good chance of a medal this year, a very good chance. Anyways, I shall have my hands full with the colt."

So Denis led Black Diamond around and around the Judging Ring. He watched the other competitors carefully to know what to do, and walked so that the judges could admire the horse's stately tread, the great feathery feet that never trod on Denis's toes, and the corded muscles of the arched neck. Then he ran, and Black Diamond lifted his knees so that his feet rose up and down like pistons, and the plumes nodded above his great gentle head.

"First Prize to Black Diamond," said the judges, so then Denis had to lead Black Diamond at the head of all the animals in the show right around the big ring for the Grand Parade.

Afterward, he sat on the grass with the farmer's family, for he felt like one of them now, and ate bacon sandwiches and lettuce and huge slices of cream-filled sponge cake and strawberries, and washed it all down with cider. "Thanks at lot, son," said the farmer, afterward, and gave him a five-pound note. "Go and

75

enjoy yourself now—but if ever you want a job on a farm, you know where to come. I shall expect you next year, mind!"

Even five pounds does not last forever when there is so much to spend it on, and eventually Denis found himself standing by the bumper cars with not a penny left.

"Hey, you," said the man in charge. "I seen you in the Grand Parade. You seem a sensible lad. Could you take over from Charlie here while he goes and gets a bite to eat?"

Charlie's job was to take the money from the passengers in the bumper cars, and to help any of them who got stuck. Denis had noticed that he also gave himself free trips if one of the cars happened to be empty.

"Yeah, O.K.," he said. He soon learned how to climb across from car to car and sort out traffic jams, or disconnect a car that had failed and steer it to the side, and how to operate the emergency lever to bring everyone to a halt in an emergency. Things were pretty busy, because it was evening by now, and children had been out of school long enough to come from quite far away.

"Hello!" said a voice. "How did you get this job?" It was Emma, with her four-year-old brother. Denis gave them the car he knew went best, but after a while he saw they were in trouble, because two boys were making a dead set at Emma's car, deliberately crashing into it again and again. The little brother was getting frightened, and crying, and Emma was looking like crying, too, for she could not protect her brother from the jolts and steer the car as well. Denis leaped across the moving cars.

"You stop that!" he shouted. "It's not allowed." But they were bigger than him, and did not stop. Denis went and pulled the lever, and everything stopped. "Out, you two," he said, in the sudden silence. The boys were startled, and looking round saw the

76

man in charge, a big burly fellow, coming over to see what was up. They leaped from the car and ran off among the crowds. Denis pulled the lever once more and the cars burst into life again.

"Quite right, sonny," said a fat woman nearby. "They didn't ought to be allowed to do that."

"They can't while I'm around," said Denis.

When Charlie came back, the man in charge gave Denis a free pass to go on all the things in the fairground. It enabled him to go on the flying boats with Emma, who was afraid to go by herself with her little brother, because he needed to have someone on each side of him to keep him safe. He lent his free pass to the brother to go on the tiny ones' train, and they watched him go around and around while Denis licked the candy floss that Emma bought him in exchange.

Then Emma had to go home, but Denis went to watch the motorbike racing.

Suddenly, just as the machines came skidding around the corner toward their part of the ring, a toddler staggered out from under the rail and tottered, giggling and unsteady, straight into the paths of the cyclists. Quick as lightning, Denis slipped out after him, and raced to pick him up. There was no time to run back with him; all he could do was stand quite still, clutching the child, and let the machines roar past him on either side. A frantic father rushed out to meet him as he returned.

"It's all right," said Denis, nonchalantly, and disappeared into the crowd. A little later, he heard the voice over the loudspeaker asking for the boy whose quick thinking had saved a child's life to come to the commentary box so that they could announce his name and give him a reward.

Denis was about to go, but then he stopped. He had been so happy all day he didn't need any reward. He'd been treated so kindly by so many people he didn't want any more fuss. It was time for the last train home, and he went quietly off and caught it.

Next day was awful, despite the fact that Mr. Hornet continued that day and every day to be kind and cheerful, quite unlike his own self. Despite, too, Emma's tale to her friends of how she had met Denis at Biddleton Show and he'd been quite different from the Dregs they all knew at school. All that Denis could think about was that he had had his happy day and he would never have another. Unless, that is, he swallowed the other red pearl, and finished the chain of happiness for good, for the sake of one more happy day.

He could neither bring himself to do that, nor give it away, so he just went on being miserable, and scruffy, and ashamed, day after day after day. Anyway, he couldn't think whom to give it *to*. Someone who needed it, Mr. Hornet had said. That ruled out Emma. There wasn't anyone else he wanted to make happy.

The new baby at home made matters worse. The little house was always full of bottles and nappies and squawking infant, and the three-year-old was always demanding attention, not wanting to be left out. One evening, Denis was driven to revive an old habit, and go to watch television at Nellie Maggs's. He had scarcely spoken to her since the stone throwing incident but he supposed she would welcome him with the usual wide grin.

He found Nellie Maggs lying on her back among the pansies, with teardrops in the wrinkles of her cheeks.

"Nellie! Are you hurt?"

"Oh, Denis, lovey, thank God you've come. No, I'm not hurt— just overbalanced, and these stupid old legs— I just can't seem able to get myself turned over so as I can get up." She attempted her grin.

Denis heaved her up and helped her sit on the doorstep. "How long have you been there?" he asked. Her woolly cardigan was covered all over with bits of leaves, and earth.

"Lord, don't ask me. I done a bit of weeding, while I was down, and a bit of struggling, and a bit of cursing. But mostly I just been lying on my back watching that old seagull and wishing I was him. Always wanted to fly." She patted the ugly bent legs. "Daft, aren't I? All those fairy stories we used to read together—remember them? Wish for this, wish for that. . . ."

"Wait," said Denis. "I got something for you." He ran quickly around to his own garden, pulled out the loose half-brick in the wall that hid the sugar-lump box, and was back before he had time to change his mind. "This might help you to fly," he said. "One way or another."

Next morning, Nellie was gone from her cottage, which didn't surprise Denis. From the school playground he gazed up at a wheeling seagull, and wondered if it was Nellie Maggs. He said as much to Mr. Hornet, for he found that now, for the first time, he could talk about the happy day to Mr. Hornet. Indeed, he was so happy, all the time, that he could talk to anyone, but the red-gold pearl was a secret between him and Mr. Hornet—and soon Nellie Maggs, for he had a feeling that she wouldn't be so stupid as to try to hang onto that second happy day, as he and Mr. Hornet had done.

"Could be," said Mr. Hornet. "But I didn't find it made that sort of magic, did you?"

"No," said Denis. "In fact, it might not have *been* magic. It could all have happened anyway."

Spring-heeled Jack

BY GWEN GRANT

To Anna, the day they moved was the most exciting of her life.

She raced up and down with pictures and pans and odd things that had been left out of boxes.

At last, it was finished. The apartment was empty and the bare rooms looked slightly tawdry with everything done. The rain lashed the wide windows and Anna closed the door behind her, glad they were leaving.

Her mother fussed about the times of the buses.

"If we get one straight into town, we'll be at the house in oh, what, fifteen minutes? Yes, fifteen minutes. Come on, Anna. We'll have to get a move on."

They hurried along the desolate street. Because of the rain, none of Anna's friends were out playing and her mother had kept her too busy to go around knocking on doors and saying goodbye.

"It isn't as if you're going to the end of the world," her mother said. "You'll probably see them just as often," but Anna had a feeling she wouldn't.

Despite everything, she could only feel pleased they were moving.

She looked back once. The apartment building sat in its place in the row of buildings. They looked like an unimaginative Stonehenge. High up one concrete wall, she could see their bare windows, blank-faced without her mother's net curtains.

By the following week, someone else would be living there but Anna, her mother, father and brother Jason, they would be living in the small terraced house they were now making their way to.

By six o'clock the little house glowed with light and warmth. An enormous coal fire leaped and twisted up the chimney and Anna kept breaking off her work to look at it.

She had never lived where you could have a fire before, and she found it enchanting.

She'd read about making pictures in the fire and now she could do it for herself. Those pieces of coal at one side, they looked like rocks. Rocks that a determined prince would ride up perhaps, to rescue a damsel in distress. Down the sides of the black lumps, a liquid rope of fire turned into long golden tresses.

Unthinkingly, Anna ran a hand over her own plain brown braids.

"Come on, Anna. Get a move on." Her mother nudged her impatiently, splintering her daydream. "There'll be plenty of time to look in the fire when we've got sorted out a bit more," and then her eyes fell on the clock. "Look at the time," she said in breathless amazement. "The dog hasn't been for a walk yet and here I am with not a drop of milk in the house."

She crossed the small untidy room to ferret for her purse on the mantelpiece.

"Look, love," she said. "Get Toby and go down to the shop

81

at the bottom of the road and get us a pint of milk. Kill two birds with one stone, that way."

Anna put her hooded dufflecoat on and tied a blue and white striped scarf round her neck.

"Come on, Tobe," she called to the nervous dog, who was looking for his vanished basket.

"Poor old Tobe," she crooned, patting his rough head.

When Toby saw the lead, he forgot about his missing bed and started to jump. Outside lay a whole new world and it was one he couldn't wait to investigate.

Anna opened the old wooden door carefully. She was used to a modern glass door with metal leaves curling its way up the frosted panel, but she liked the old door. It wasn't a very nice color. Dark green.

"Hospital paint that," her dad said. "Probably giving it away. Can't imagine anybody buying that color, can you, Jean?" he asked his wife and she looked around the dark green kitchen and thought of the dark green bathroom and dark green back bedroom and nodded her head.

"Wherever it came from," she said. "I wish it hadn't."

"Shan't be long," Anna said, looking up at her dad standing in the doorway, the light behind him making him seem cut out of the night.

"And watch your step," he called. "Don't talk to no strangers and come straight back."

"I'll be all right, Dad," Anna said and she and Toby walked down the street.

At first Anna was so busy looking around her, she found the darkness didn't bother her at all.

Theirs was a shortish street leading onto a much longer street of houses that tumbled down a steep hill. Two houses and a long dark passage. Two houses and a long dark passage. That was how they were set out.

It was only drizzling now and Anna's feet squelched wetly on the shining pavement. Toby hurried along, nose to the ground, somehow managing to pick up an interesting smell every now and again despite the rain.

It was while Anna was walking past one of the passages that she thought she saw a movement out of the corner of her eye. She turned her head sharply but there was no one there. No one that she could see, anyway.

The dark gaping mouth of the passage stared back blindly.

Anna took a deep breath and shook herself sternly.

"You're just frightening yourself for nothing," she said to Toby in a sharp voice.

Toby looked up, his head on one side.

"There's nothing there, old Tobe, is there?" Anna asked the dog and the dog stared down the passage, curled his top lip back and started to snarl. The snarl turned into a choking wail as he pulled on the lead, his head straining toward the dark hole.

Anna pulled him back, hesitated a second and then took to her heels. She flew down the street, Toby running unwillingly alongside her. She could feel the dog's head turning as he pulled on the lead but she kept running.

In two short minutes, she was standing in the safety of the lighted shop doorway.

Anna leaned against the shop window, her breath catching in her throat. Her heart was beating so heavily, it hurt.

After a minute or two, she felt able to go into the shop. The woman behind the counter stared at her but all she saw was a girl with cheeks rosy from running, her hair beaded with silvery specks of rain where the duffle hood had fallen back from her face.

"Evening," the woman said and Anna wondered if she should tell her about the passage, but tell her what? She hadn't seen anything. It was only Toby who'd growled and carried on.

She bought the pint of milk and put it in the shopping bag her mother had given her.

When she was out of the shop, she looked up the long dark hilly street and blazed with relief to see her brother walking toward her.

"Dad sent me to meet you," he grumbled. "Dunno why. There's not much can happen between here and home."

"I don't know about that," Anna said weakly and told Jason about the passageway.

"Probably a cat," he shrugged. "You know what Toby is for cats," and Anna laughed.

Of course, she thought, why hadn't she realized it was probably a cat.

They walked up the street, chattering about the day. About how different these small dark streets were from the wide orange-lit streets of the old neighborhood. They walked past lighted windows which were only slightly taller than themselves.

"I really like this," Toby said. "You look up and all you see is sky. No windows staring down at you like in the apartments."

"And nobody throwing things at you either," Anna replied.

They were so engrossed in their talk that the only warning they had was when Toby sprang forward on his lead, barking wildly.

In front of them, near enough to be touched, a giant shadow catapulted out of a passageway. The shadow flew high in the air, came down heavily, bent until it was half its size and then, with another leap, had vanished.

Anna saw a monstrous creature, dark as the night itself, in front of her. It seemed to jump as high as the houses. She felt her cheek grazed by the flick of a hard material. Then the giant became a dwarf whose pale oval face was almost on a level with Anna's. She caught a glimpse of spiteful bright eyes and then the face was gone.

84

It happened so quickly and so soundlessly that the two children were still gaping at where the apparition had been by the time it had gone. They hadn't even had a chance to move their positions.

And then Anna opened her mouth and screamed and screamed and screamed, while Jason, white-faced, tried to comfort her.

The street came alive with noise and people. Lights went on, doors flew open, people fell out of their houses, all exclaiming and asking questions.

"Who?" "What?" "Why?" "Where?" "When?" they called, shouted and demanded.

They quickly had the story out of the two children but it turned out to be an old story.

"Spring-heeled Jack," they said angrily and the men got together in a tense crowd.

The police came. The people were sent home, Anna and Jason taken home.

"He doesn't do anything," the policeman told their parents. "All he does is jump out and then disappear."

"He was a giant," Anna wailed.

"Massive," Jason agreed. "But little too," and Anna thought of those white eyes staring into hers and she shuddered.

The men were going to search the streets. The police were in and out of the passages and back gardens but after a thorough look, they came up empty-handed.

"Never find anything," Anna heard. "He comes and goes like a blooming ghost."

"There's nothing ghostly about this graze on my daughter's face," Anna's mother said tartly.

The days passed. The memory of Spring-heeled Jack lessened a little, her cheek started to heal and Anna went to bed more easily. She started to treat the small streets with caution.

From time to time, they heard of more jumpings. The lodger next door said, "It's since they pulled down the old church, I tell you. If you asks me, they let something out of there." Anna, looking at him, felt a slight sense of recognition.

Recoiling from the lodger, she dodged behind her father's back.

The lodger's mouth curved in a smile but he never smiled directly at anyone with his eyes. He always smiled at the floor.

Anna's mother glanced sharply at the man but he held his tea cup so carefully. He put it on the table so gently. He seemed a gray, careful, gentle man.

Anna asked if anyone had a picture of the old church and the lodger said he had.

"I'll get it for you," he said and came back with it held tightly in his thick fingers.

The girl studied the picture intently, going back to it again and again.

The lodger smiled as he watched her.

Later that evening when Anna and her mother walked past the waste ground where the church had once stood, Anna said, "Do you think the lodger's telling the truth?"

"What?" said her mother. "About the church? Lot of nonsense. Ought to have more sense, scaring folk half to death. I'll have a word with him," she finished, angry again as she remembered the lodger's words and saw her daughter's strained face.

Anna stared at the waste ground all the time they were walking past it. The land was dark and deserted. She shivered and turned her head but a flickering point of light drew her attention. She looked away but had to look back. It was still there.

"Mom," she whispered. "Look. That light," and her mother turned and looked.

"Where?" she said.

"There," Anna pointed.

The light was like Spring-heeled Jack. One minute it seemed large. The next, it almost disappeared.

"My word," her mother said crossly. "We'll see about this," and she moved toward the nearest house. "We'll get some help, Anna, and go and see exactly what's going on there."

The people in the house got other people and they all went to see what the light was.

It was just a candle, pressed into the earth, burning. Beside it lay an untidy scattering of gray stone.

"Why, it looks like an altar candle," a man said, leaving the long white candle where it was. "Steal anything these days they will. Anything that isn't tied down. Steal the breath out of your mouth if they could."

Anna flinched as she thought of someone stealing the breath from her mouth.

She moved the stones with her foot then turned away.

"I'll wait over here," she told her mother, and made her way back across the waste land. Back to the street and the lamp posts.

She had almost reached the pavement when she felt a prickling on her skin.

Sharply, she turned around and there, standing against the dark wall, was a black shadow. The next instant, Spring-heeled Jack lurched toward her and then his familiar movements appeared. Anna saw the dark shape leap up into the air and it seemed as if he had taken her breath after all, because when Anna tried to scream, no sound came out of her open mouth.

By the candle, someone glanced over.

"It's him," they shouted. "It's him." And a stream of people poured across the rough, uneven land.

They put Anna to bed with a glass of hot milk and a pill from the doctor.

"They didn't catch him, did they?" she asked harshly.

Her mother shook her head.

"He's after me," Anna cried. "Why? What does he want? Why is he picking on me?"

87

Her parents looked helplessly at each other. The move was going wrong.

"We should have stayed where we were," her mother said and locked the doors and drew the curtains. "Nothing like this ever happened in the apartments."

Every night now, the men in the streets roamed up and down but they were almost as frightening as Spring-heeled Jack if you didn't see them hiding, waiting. To look down a passage and see the quiet lighted end of a cigarette wasn't always the comfort the men meant it to be.

The lodger appeared at the back door to ask, "How's the child today?"

Anna's mother retorted sharply, "Very well. Very well," and the lodger's plasticine gray face folded itself about with satisfaction.

Anna sat in a chair, well wrapped up against the cold and the chill of fear that was in her body. She had slept and now she woke as the lodger's voice broke through her sleep.

She turned her eyes on him and followed the curved-down smile. The sense of recognition overwhelmed her tantalizingly.

As if feeling her gaze, the lodger looked straight at her and his malicious flickering eyes stared briefly into hers.

"Still using the picture of the old church, are you?" he asked, his voice sounding as ancient and rusty as an old key in a lock.

Anna nodded.

The lodger murmured softly and was gone.

Anna reached for the picture and concentrated her attention upon it. Thoughtfully, she traced the printed stonework with her finger. Suddenly, an almost hidden detail leaped out at her. Her breath caught in her throat and she let the picture fall to her knee.

Later that day, Anna made her pilgrimage to the waste ground.

The thin winter sun played at shadows with the ivy climbing over the rubble.

Anna walked through the old church land and stopped where she thought the candle would have been. She knelt down and moved the debris around with her fingertips, carefully, carefully.

She went in a wider and wider circle and then, pulling back the straggling stems of a clump of weeds, she found what she was looking for.

She picked it up and held it in her hands. The malicious stone face smiled back at her. A gargoyle displaced.

Anna stared somberly at the grotesque head. She took it down to the old priory in the town and left it on the font, close to a source of the water that was its life's blood, and where it was sure to be found.

In her mind, she could hear the lodger.

"It's since they pulled down the old church. They let something out of there."

Well, Anna thought, brushing the gray dust off her hands. Now they've got it back.

And maybe they had.

Anyway, no one ever heard of Spring-heeled Jack again.

The Demon Kite

BY FARRUKH DHONDY

MAHYAR LIVED IN A LARGE HOUSE SURROUNDED BY A
spacious garden. Outside his front gate ran the main road and
across the road there was a huge field known to all the people
of the town as the *maidan*. Mahyar's father was very rich, he
was the Director of the Devi Cotton Mills. In their house they
had seven servants, counting the chauffeur who was paid by the
mill to drive Mahyar's father and his family around in the two
cars which they owned.

On Saturday Mahyar's friends would come to his house,
friends he made in the exclusive school to which he went. On
weekdays Mahyar was alone. He'd do his homework and sometimes he'd go to the *maidan* with the young servant who ran
errands for the cook and the bearer, whom everyone called Boy.

The most popular game of the hot months was kite fights. The
poor boys of the city would gather in the *maidan* in pairs and
gangs and fly kites. The sky above the *maidan* would be dotted
with the colors of the tissue paper stretched on a cross of bamboo

sticks. If you actually stood next to the flyers, you could see the cat's cradle of threads, all tense and colored, making a skein across the sky. The thread of the kites was not just ordinary thread. It was made by passing number-ten-thickness cotton through a hot can full of gelatin and crushed glass. The thread was dipped through this sticky, lethal mixture and left out in the sun to dry. When it was dry, it was deadly. If you ran it through your fingers and held your finger tight around it, the greens and blues of the cotton would come away crimson with your blood. The flyers would launch their kites into the sky and bring them down and the thread of one kit would graze against the thread of another and the sharp, glassy length would cut through the thread of the opposing kite.

Mahyar had lost a few kite fights himself. Boy had held the reel of glassed thread as Mahyar manipulated his kite across the sky, reeling and dipping and challenging the others on the *maidan*. He knew the heavy pull of the expensive kite when it got to the upper reaches of the breeze. He knew the sudden lightness, the limp and defeated feeling when his own kite was cut.

The kites which were cut floated away. They were chased by the boys on the *maidan* who brandished branches of trees and long bamboo sticks to entangle the thread of the cut kite and catch it and claim it for themselves.

The champion flyer in all the *maidan* was a boy named Datta. Datta was a poor boy and he didn't have any money to buy kites for himself, but he always had a a kite to fly because he made it his business to chase the cut kites and claim them when he caught them.

Mahyar knew the names of all the different varieties of kite that flew in the *maidan*. His friends from school didn't know such things. If they flew kites, they flew them with the help of their fathers or servants from the terraces of their houses, far away from where the poor boys gathered for the great game. Mahyar knew that the kite with two balanced triangles was called a *bhowra*, a top; the one with a central piece and two triangular fins on either side was called a *machhli*, a fish; and a single colored one was called a *rangi*, a colored one.

One evening at the end of the hot season a strange kite appeared in the sky above the *maidan*. Mahyar was sitting in his room doing his homework. He was doing fractions and feeling quite proud that he knew his seventeen times table so well that his teacher had asked him to start writing in an ordinary lined book instead of in the squared ones they used in the lower classes.

Just then Boy rushed up.

"Have you seen the *patang*, Mahyar *baba*," he said. "The kite, it's like a second sun in the sky. Nobody knows who's flying it. It's got a straight thread and it's coming from far across the trees in Koregaon Park. Just like an electric wire, strong like that."

"Wait two minutes for me," Mahyar said, "and wait quietly because seven seventeens are 119 plus four which gives 123." Mahyar put his pen down. He leaned out of the window for a good look.

The kite was very high up now and several others rose from the *maidan* to challenge it. It's colors were very clear. It was red with a pattern of crescent moons in yellow and blue and black near its four corners. It was a diamond shape and not the usual stretched square. It had two drooping mustaches of silver hanging over the smile of the bottom crescent.

"Let's go," Mahyar said, and he and Boy ran out of the house and out of the gate and into the *maidan*.

From the *maidan* he thought he could see the light of the sun bouncing off the surface of the kite, like a mirror throwing flashes over the crowd. The thread of the kite was purple and it glistened with what looked like globules of very shiny glass.

92

"Maybe someone is flying it from a terrace in Bund Garden Road," Mahyar said.

"Not possible," Boy said, "Datta's men have even cycled out to find where it's coming from and they said it goes beyond the hills even, right over the town."

"Don't be idiotic."

"Yes, I'm telling you, it goes on and on like a railway line."

Mahyar saw two other kites ascend from different ends of the field. One large blue and green *bhowra* was clearly intent on a fight. The crowd gave a little shout as the *"page,"* the kite fight, commenced. The *bhowra* was sent gliding slowly out and then brought with a jerk into a dive onto the thread of the alien kite and then released again. It quivered in the wind. For a whole second it hesitated as thread met thread and then floated away on the wind like a hand waving goodbye. The crowd shouted again. The flyer had dropped his reel of thread and was running across the *maidan*, together with fifty other boys, to retrieve the cut kite.

"It has to be soda thread," Mahyar said.

Then he spotted Datta who stood in a cluster of boys. They weren't going to run for the kite. It was funny. One of the boys from the gang heard Mahyar's remark to Boy about the thread.

"What soda thread," he said. "It's got electric thread, every time it cuts a kite, some sparks come out of it."

"It's a demon kite," Datta said. "Demons have to be brought down."

He was staring at the crescent wonder, standing fixed on the grass of the *maidan* in bare feet, his legs sticking out of the threadbare, rolled-up hems of his cotton trousers.

Mahyar knew that the boys in his gang were waiting for Datta's word.

"I've seen demon kites before. Slowly, day after day it'll rake the stiffness out of the breeze over our *maidan*. We'll never be able to fly kites here again." Datta was quite firm about what he said. The twilight was fast upon them.

"Why are we standing here? We can catch all the kites that the demon cuts," one of the boys in the gang said.

"You first-born always talk like idiots," Datta said. "Once a kite has been cut by the demon kite, it's good for nothing; it won't take the wind. You watch."

As he spoke the demon kite began to glide slowly further away from where they stood. It moved steadily, as though it were a cousin of the clouds themselves.

"We'll get some wire tomorrow if it's still here, and tie it to stones and bring the devil down."

"Where's it going?" Boy asked. He was addressing his question to Datta.

"It's looking for your sister," one of the other boys said.

"It's going where the sun hasn't yet set," Datta said.

Over dinner Mahyar told his dad about the demon kite. Only he didn't say it was a demon kite. That sort of talk was not tolerated in the house. His dad said that someone was probably flying it from the water tower, because that was the highest point in town.

"Some boys were saying it's a demon kite," Mahyar said.

"Uneducated people. They'll believe anything," his father said.

The next day in school Mahyar thought about the kite. . . . He'd looked for it in the morning, out of the window of the car, but it wasn't above the *maidan*. He didn't say a word about it to his school friends, because they'd laugh at him for believing what the street boys believed.

The kite became a beacon in the evening sky. Everyone now knew that it was a very powerful kite, the strongest they had ever seen, but most believed that it was being flown from the water tower. Some of the regular gangs of the *maidan* began to ignore the demon kite and fight their own battles in the far corner. Mahyar would stay in his room and after finishing his homework he would sit at the window and watch the demon kite from there, dancing, curving, diving like a swallow, seeming to show off now to try and attract attention it had lost by standing still. Mahyar could see that Datta's gang was no longer with him. They darted about the *maidan* with branches and bamboos.

Mahyar thought about the kite a lot. He knew that Datta was thinking about it too. If Datta was right and it was a demon kite, then possessing it would give him power over the whole *maidan*. It would be something like possessing a death-ray pistol, or like having Batman as your personal friend.

Then the rains came. When the rains actually came down hard, Mahyar saw that people were more bothered about keeping themselves dry than about watching the antics of the demon kite.

Mahyar had stopped going to the *maidan*; he was playing records on the portable player that his father had bought him. He glanced out of the window beyond the sleepy weepy roots of the banyan tree. The *maidan* was deserted; he could see a lone figure standing in the center of the field. It was Datta, standing there with his kite-catching branch looking up at the sky. Mahyar looked up automatically, searching the sky for the demon kite, but it was no longer there. Not even a demon flyer would launch a kite into a sky full of black clouds. Datta had gone crazy. Even Boy said he'd gone crazy and that's why his gang had left him.

Then it caught his eye. As he turned away from the record player, Mahyar could see the demon kite low in the center of the *maidan*. He was surprised. It couldn't have flown on the wind that fast. Why had its flyer launched it? Was there a flyer? There weren't any other kites that evening, only the black clouds, scattered and frowning and threatening to gang together and storm down. Then a thought struck Mahyar. The kite had come to challenge the clouds. Stupid. It seemed closer than it had been before and he could see funny patterns, like writing in a strange language around its crescent moons.

Mahyar noticed that the light was dying and clouds came on thicker from over the trees and yet the demon kite looked brighter than it ever had. It's better go back from where it had come, he thought. He saw Datta following its progress across the *maidan* and upward toward the clouds. Then just as the rain began to fall, there was the crash of distant thunder. The drops fell on the leaves of the banyan tree and made a sound like an army marching. Datta still stood in the center of the field, absolutely still.

The kite was still climbing, reaching up to the clouds. And it shone and the silver writing around the crescents looked like writhing snakes as it glistened. It's not beautiful, Mahyar thought, it's really a demon kite. He couldn't see its thread even though he strained his eyes. It was getting dark fast. Then a flash of lightning shot from the clouds just above the kite. Mahyar was amazed. In the flash he saw the purple thread of the kite, and he thought he saw it being hit by the lightning. He was right. The kite turned like a person falling backward. It hit the wind horizontally and then like any other kite separated from its flyer, it began to glide on the layers of air.

As he looked out of the window, Mahyar was sure that no one but he and Datta had seen the demon kite's fight with the lightning. Datta was beginning to run. Mahyar felt his heart pounding. He dashed out of this room, down the stairs and into the garden. In a moment he was across the street and on the *maidan*. Maybe I should get a bamboo out of the garage, he thought, Datta has a branch. But his feet were faster than his thoughts. I've got to catch it, I've got to fight to catch it, he was thinking.

He looked up and saw that the kite was coming to him. So was Datta. The kite flew low now. It was bigger than he'd thought. It had a huge grin on its face. It was steadily coming down. Mahyar sighted its thread that trailed behind, a long loop disappearing into the grass thirty yards from him.

Mahyar stopped running. All Mahyar had to do was wait till the thread glided over him and grab it. He'd won the race.

He waited and then leaped for the thread, losing sight of the kite which was at the edge of the *maidan* near the road. All he could see now was the glitter of the thread and he felt it rasping through his closed fist. Mayhar grabbed it and began hauling it in across the grass, trying to pull in as much of the loose trail before Datta got to it. He wrapped it frantically around his left arm and he turned to see where the kite had glided. Just as he felt the weight of the kite on the thread, he was aware of the panting breath of Datta on him.

"Leave that thread go, slippery little brat," Datta said.

"I caught it first," Mahyar said. "It's mine, I've got it. I caught this kite."

"You give me that thread," Datta said.

"No, it's mine," Mahyar said as he ran after the kite which was slowly, majestically crossing the road. Datta grabbed for the thread. Suddenly Mahyar realized that to Datta it wasn't a game. Winning and losing were part of a game but the catching of the demon kite was not a game. As they crossed the street together, jostling and digging each other in the ribs, they could see the demon kite hesitating on the air. Then it sliced itself in one smooth sweep into Mahyar's garden and the waiting branches of the banyan tree. There it hung, horizontal and lethargic. The thread in Mahyar's hand went limp. Datta's hand grabbed Mahyar's wrist and the purple thread wrapped around it. It a deft movement, Datta caught the thread beyond Mahyar's arm and snapped it.

"It's my kite, it's in my tree, I caught it fair and square," Mahyar said.

Datta wasn't paying any attention. He had run up to the garden wall and was trying to jerk the kite out of its perch in the tree.

"That's my house," Mahyar said.

Datta was looking around with the practiced look of a boy who scaled walls and ran the risks that private gardens offered.

Mahyar ran toward the gate. At least he'd be the first up the tree. As he reached it he could see that Datta had climbed on top of the wall and was jerking at the thread frantically. Mahyar could hear the paper of the kite thrashing about against the leaves of the banyan tree.

"I'll call my servants," Mahyar said.

He heard Datta laugh. Datta was jerking harder now and though neither of them could see where the kite had disappeared in the thick foliage of the banyan tree, they could hear it. It was like birds having a fight.

"Don't you have any respect for the demon kite?"

"What demon kite, it's just an ordinary kite. If you're going to call your servants, I'll tear it up from here before I run."

"Suppose I give you some money?"

"For what?"

"For leaving it alone."

"How much?"

"Four rupees."

"Where's the money?"

"If you give me the thread I'll get it."

"All right, four rupees for the thread."

Mahyar turned, ran upstairs to his room and pulled the notes out of the leather wallet in his chest of drawers. He counted four rupees as he ran out again. He held the notes up to Datta who took them, tucked them in his trousers and jumped off the wall onto the road. Without a word of thanks to Mahyar, he crossed the road, picked up his kite-catching branch and disappeared onto the dark of the *maidan*. Mahyar watched him go.

The kite was his now. He'd take it down in the morning. It was the first kite he'd ever caught. He wouldn't tell Boy about the kite, he'd just get up early and climb and get it and paper over any cracks and tears it might have suffered. Then in the evening he'd take it to the terrace and fly it. He wouldn't risk going to the *maidan*. The boys on the *maidan* would all look up and see him flying the demon kite and they wouldn't know how it had fallen from its pedestal in the sky into his hands.

He slept lightly that night and woke up to what he thought were footsteps on the gravel outside. The window, which he'd left open, was lit by the moon. Mahyar lay under the quilt and listened. There was some sound outside. He got out of bed and went to the window. A sight awaited him. The demon kite had loosened itself from the upper branches and hung a few yards from his window. The kite shone in the moonlight and cast a glow around itself. Mahyar scratched himself on the thigh through his pajamas to make sure he was awake.

The red of the demon kite looked like the color of ripe watermelon. The crescents grinned. The colors in the crescents began to look to Mahyar like the teeth of a smile; the patterns around them, silver and gray, like a haze cast around the paper. As he stared at it, it looked to him like the sail of a pirate ship with a skull spread over it; then it looked red and blue and shone with golden streaks like the fan of a peacock, and still he looked at it and he thought it changed as he looked, into the tawny face of an owl. The demon kite fluttered, and its motion was like the sweep of a curtain hanging in the doorway of some palace in a desert; and then it looked to him like the standard borne in the air by the bearers of a barbarian chief leading an army on horseback; a mask work by a dancer; the face of a wise man from

China; a basket of striped snakes; a rider plunging over the moon; a drowned galleon; the sad eyes of a prince who has lost an empire; the pattern of a cobweb; a car on a mountain railway in a stormy night; a hanged man.

The kite dangled just three yards away from his reach in the leaves of the banyan tree. Mahyar realized that the thud and crunch he'd heard were real footsteps. He looked away from the kite as he heard the rustling of the branches and he saw the silhouette of a boy climbing the forks and knuckles of the tree toward were the kite hung. He wanted to cry out but he didn't because the night was too silent for his voice to disturb. He knew it was Datta.

As Datta reached the coil of thread which held the kite to the tree, Mahyar saw the sharp sheen of a switchblade knife.

"I thought I bought that kite from you." His voice came out in a pleading whisper.

"You think you can buy anything? Call the police if you like," Datta said, cutting the demon kite loose from its harness. Datta began to climb down the tree again.

"Datta," Mahyar said.

"So you know my name, then, slippery."

"You know I caught it first. I got the thread before you."

"I'm not playing that game anymore," Datta said.

"I'll give you five more rupees."

"What? Five rupees for a demon kite?"

"You said it wasn't a demon kite."

Datta was now at the bottom of the tree picking up the kite and winding the loose thread in a figure eight on his outstretched thumb and little finger. Mahyar knew there was nothing he could do to stop him. Even so, the words came out of his mouth.

"How much do you want for it?"

"You can't fly this kite from your terrace. It doesn't belong in

100

your garden or to you. Ask your father to buy you one from the bazaar. Only a demon flyer can make this a demon kite again." Datta said, hauling the kite over his shoulder like a great cape, and Mahyar caught the glint of the moon shining from his eyes as he turned and made for the gate.

The Book of the Black Arts

BY PATRICIA MILES

"Yes, but what is it exactly?" Cheryl asked.

"See for yourself." The man smiled and pushed the book gently toward her, avoiding the other books stacked in heaps all around. A strange aroma came with him. He smelled faintly of wet toast.

Cheryl glanced up at him. He had black hair, and his eyebrows quirked up in the middle like circumflex accents. He looked foreign or something, she thought. Perhaps he was the French teacher. *She* didn't know—it was her brother's school, all decked out for its Christmas fair.

"We get the oddest things to sell," he said.

It was a large book, bound in black leather. You could fasten it up with gilt clasps, like an old Bible.

Cheryl shivered. The stall must be at the draftiest end of the hall. There was no one near it but herself and two small boys hunting through a box of tattered comics. They seemed to feel the cold too, and in a moment jumped up and ran off.

She undid the clasps, raised the cover, and loked at the title. "The Book of the Black Arts," she read aloud—and gave a surprised laugh.

"Handle it," said the teacher, or whatever. "Look inside." A touch of keenness had crept into his voice, but when he finished speaking he closed his lips and waited. She turned the pages.

"It's like a diary," she said doubtfully. The pages were thick and good, but empty. They had rich black borders, of leaves and flowers. Here and there she saw writing, but when she flicked back she wasn't able to find it again. "It's not a diary, though, is it?"

He shook his head. "Not exactly."

She picked it up. It was quite heavy.

"What *is* it for, really?"

"It's for getting what you want. You write it down and it comes." He caught her eye. "I'm serious," he said.

She felt an immediate surge of greed. She could have a new bike, roller skates, a videotape recorder!

"What's that? What have you got there?" said Brigine, bounding up. She was the same age as Cheryl—thirteen.

"You can have anything you like," the man continued, "wealth! power! Just put it in the book."

"Oh, what fun!" And as Cheryl stood hesitating, Brigine took it out of her hands.

Cheryl sensed a shift in his interest. This was normal for anyone who was a friend of Brigine. Brigine had chestnut hair and gray-green eyes. Her skin put you in mind of some very superior form of color photography. On top of all that she had personality, lots of it—and she wasn't bad at the violin.

"I'll have it," she said. "How much?"

"Five pence."

"Honestly? Don't you think you could get a bit more for it than that?"

The man shrugged. "It's far from new," he said. "Oh, and

there is one thing. I'd rather not take copper. Now, you're sure you want it?"

Cheryl spoke up. "There's a catch, isn't there? There must be."

"Naturally." His smile broadened. "Just the usual sort of thing. You can't give it away; you have to sell it for a price smaller than what you paid—that's why you're getting it so cheap. Silver coins only, by the way. Oh, and if you should happen to die with it still in your keeping, I'm afraid—ha, ha—the devil gets you. Your soul goes straight to hell."

Hell—his lips twitched after he said it, and his arched eyebrows shot up in a humorous way.

Brigine smiled back at him. Hell? The Devil? Who believed in them? She got out her purse. She felt Cheryl tug at her jacket, but she ignored her, and handed over a five-pence coin.

He took out a pen. "Put your name in the book. You have to do that."

"Really?" For the first time she slowed down in her headlong rush. "Why?"

"Why not? If it get you what you want. You could even be famous," he added jollily.

She took the pen. "My name's Brigine. The *g* is soft. A lot of people don't get it right."

"I expect they soon will."

She wrote it in neatly, "Brigine Damant."

Cheryl stood back. She felt sorry, half relieved. Then, rubbing her hands against the cold, she caught a snatch of someone else's conversation: "Fog? Yes, it's getting quite foggy."

"Come on, Brigine. I've had enough of this. Let's go," she said.

They collected Steven, her young brother. "Who is that teacher?" Cheryl asked, as they were leaving. Steven glanced back at the bookstall and shrugged. "Dunno, not one of ours. Must be one of the parents," he said indifferently.

Outside, the streetlights were wreathed in mist. They hurried along the greasy sidewalks, sniffing in the tarry smell of the fog. Lit windows looked inviting and homely.

"That man," said Cheryl suddenly. "You don't believe it, do you—what he said?"

"Course not," answered Brigine.

"What are you talking about?" Steven asked. Both girls ignored him.

"I'd like another look at it," said Cheryl. "Are you coming in?"

"Can't," replied Brigine, quick as a flash. "I've got orchestra tonight. Dress rehearsal."

In her room, a messy area in a small but tidy house, Brigine chucked the book on the bed and flopped down on her bean bag chair. She eyed the book. "I don't believe a word of it," she thought. But actually, she did. Just a little. Enough to try it.

There was a pen under the bed. She retrieved it, opened the book at random, and wrote in her usual neat hand:

One Thousand Pounds

and, as an afterthought:

Please.

She was extremely unprepared for her mother bursting in. She pushed the book under the quilt, but Mrs. Damant hadn't noticed; she was full of her own concerns.

"I've got to go into town—my washing machine's broken. And haven't you got orchestra?"

"Oh—oh, no. I can't go. I forgot to tell you. It's my violin. The soundpost's gone."

"Brigine!" Mrs. Damant looked annoyed. "Wait a minute, it's not much of a job, is it? If you come with me, you can get it fixed. There's a new shop, right by the launderette—but you'll have to hurry."

105

She hurried. Afterward it seemed to Brigine that one minute she was hiding the book, the next a litle old man in a music shop was hinting at something fantastic.

The violin lay between them, mended—but did she know its value, was it insured, had they had it long, where did they get it?

"My mother found it, in an auction . . . there were things damaged in a fire, but this seemed all right. She gave five pounds."

He put it back in the case. "You've been lucky," he said. "It's English, eighteenth century. I wonder if you can guess what it's really worth?"

Brigine swallowed. Her throat was dry and her hands were icy cold.

"Tell your mother, if you want to sell I can get you a thousand pounds."

"A thousand pounds?" croaked Brigine. "I'll tell her."

But she didn't. Not for some time.

That evening, after orchestra, she said: "I've asked for an audition, for the first violins. It's next Tuesday."

And in the book she wrote:

I want to be a famous violinist.

She thought for a moment, then changed it:

I want to be the world's *most* famous violinist.

She underlined "most," and didn't bother to write "please." Her heart was thumping slightly as she put down the pen.

On Tuesday she played for the conductor. He stared at her, faintly puzzled. "I don't think I'd quite realized. . . ." He roused himself. "There are one or two people who should hear you . . . and teachers . . . we'll have to think about teachers . . ."

That was the start. And the start of a life of practice—practice and more practice, five, six, seven hours a day, every day—but a wonderful life. Success came so quickly she had a feeling of being whirled away. Her star rose, but for others it was not so good—critics. Odd things happened to critics who failed to praise her. Nasty things. One critic wrote: "In her playing she is like Coppelia, or Olympia, magical dolls which perform with cold brilliance, but having no heart, no human warmth, can never achieve true greatness." The house he was living in collapsed. He was quite badly injured.

Brigine was in her twenties now. In all those years she told no one about the book. Its pages were filled with the dates of important concerts, but no one knew. She never mentioned it. Cheryl's family had moved away. They met once, at a school reunion. Brigine was already well-known, but they recognized each other and chatted.

"Whatever happened to that black book?" said Cheryl.

"Oh," said Brigine, "my mother made me get rid of it. I sold it to a Swedish girl for twenty-five öre."

"What's that?"

"About two pence."

"I'd have bought it off you," said Cheryl, with a touch of resentment.

"No, you wouldn't," said Brigine.

They looked at each other and laughed. "You're right," said Cheryl, "I wouldn't." Then with a last little dig: "I thought it might be at the back of your success."

"Did you?" Brigine gave her her dazzling celebrity smile and turned away.

Well, of course she still had it, but she wasn't going to tell *her*.

Occasionally, over the years, she saw the seller of the book, usually in some concert hall. Once from a taxi in Bayswater Road. It was the place where amateurs show their paintings on Sundays, leaning them against the railings of the park. He was talking to a middle-aged woman. He looked a little different—hair now the color of cheap tobacco, but eyebrows as quirky as ever. It was him all right. He smiled and waved his hand at Brigine and she went home and had flu for three weeks.

The flu frightened her, but naturally she couldn't give the book up now, not in the midst of her success. And then she lost it. Or rather, an airline lost it for her. It was packed away in a suitcase. The suitcase was never found, but when she was shown into her hotel suite in Rome, there the book was, on the table by the bed. She felt an enormous sense of relief, but a day later, wandering through the city, she began to wonder . . . supposing she wanted to lose it—could she? At once a queer dull heaviness seemed to spread through her, like a wave traveling through mud. No. The answer was no, she knew it was.

She had to sit down—that marble bench would do. She had reached a little park, the gardens of the Villa Wurtz. She stared dazedly at the brilliant green of the grass, at the flowers, at the children playing, and slowly began to feel better. She passed a strange peaceful half-hour in the little park, then got up, straightened her shoulders, and returned to her career.

Rome—the very stones looked warm and worldly and sinful. If she could be at ease anywhere, it was Rome. She loved it—the churches, the palaces, the fountains. And then, when she least expected it, Rome smote her a sledgehammer blow. It showed her hell.

It was a painting, a titanic, stupendous painting—sixty feet high by forty wide—and the artist was Michelangelo. It was by chance she visited the Vatican, by chance she entered the Sistine Chapel. Once there, she stood riveted to the spot, appalled by the mighty altarpiece—'The Last Judgment.' The good were there. Strong angels drew them up to Paradise, but Heaven was high up, near the ceiling, faint and far away. Hell was close, myriads of writhing bodies, slithering and tumbling down, an eye-level view—not red and fiery, but full of bluish shades and utterly chilling. She saw Hell's river, and Charon beating the dead souls out of his boat, with a skeleton or two looking on from the bank and a cold mist rising from the Styx.

She moved back, remembering a cold English evening, a Christmas fair, and haloes of chilly fog around the street lamps. Once *she* had been good—honest and loving and kind. She wished she was again.

It was raining when she came out. She returned to the hotel, took the book from its drawer, and went down to the river. Castel Sant' Angelo, squat and forbidding, glowered at her from the other side. She walked to the middle of the bridge and threw the book in. It sank. She went back. Why did her legs still feel like lead? She opened the drawer—the book was *there*. She had expected it, but seeing it was worse than just expecting it. She felt her heart, the whole world, had stopped. But—and this was the amazing thing—at the same time she wanted to pick it up and hug it. She loved it! This evil thing. Destroy the book? She must have been mad.

She approached it again slowly. It was lying open in the drawer, at a page with a list of names. She picked it up—the leather wasn't even damp—and read the last name on the list: Mrs. McGreedy.

Mrs. McGreedy, Mrs. McGreedy? She couldn't quite place it. She walked restlessly in and out of the rooms, took her violin out of its case, then put it back, and as she fastened the catch she remembered. Mrs. McGreedy was an old lady who lived near the school. She collected musical instruments. Mrs. McGreedy's house had burned down and some stuff was saved and *some was auctioned*, but Mrs. McGreedy herself died in the fire.

Madly, she went back the next day to the painting—couldn't resist it. A youngish good-looking man was staring at it, transfixed, as she had been. Brigine stood near. Tourists in groups eddied around them, came and went. At last she spoke—in English, careless of whether he understood or not.

"I don't believe in it," she said, "but it scares me."

"I don't either. Hell—or Heaven—is here, now, inside."

Brigine looked at him, deeply interested. In a moment, from posters, from newspapers, they had recognized each other, Brigine Damant and Reinhardt Mueller, the famous violinist and the famous tenor. They stood back, each appraising the other, and smiled. From then on, from that meeting, as much as their schedules would allow, they were inseparable.

"This can't be happening to me," thought Brigine. "It can't last." But for a while it did.

He showed her Vienna. She showed him Rome. And still, under all the happiness, she felt a quaking and a fear: it's too good. Too good for me.

Reinhardt went to London, to give a recital. A few days later, Brigine flew to London herself, in time for a celebration dinner.

It was quite a gathering. Reinhardt's agent, a couple of other musicians, herself—and a girl. Reinhardt had brought the girl with him. Brigine had seen her before, no one special, a young singer. But at once a jealous foreboding knocked at her heart. And later, as the meal went on, "Oh, Sylvie," he said. "You haven't got a flower." He turned to Brigine. "You can spare one, can't you?"

Rather clumsily he detached an orchid from the spray he himself had sent to her. It was an extraordinary thing to do. He gave it to Sylvie. Brigine's idyll was over.

She crawled drearily back to Rome. She wandered miserably up the Janiculum, by the Tiber, down the Spanish Steps, along the Corso. Then misery gave way to rage. At a certain point she stopped, stood still, staring at a great joyous fountain. What joy had she in anything? None. What had brought her to this? The book. She knew it now for what it was—a book of the damned.

She determined to get rid of it, not to sell it to some other unfortunate soul—she scorned the idea—but somehow to foil it and to render it harmless. What could she do? In her wanderings she had noticed a certain obscure little church. Why it appealed to her she didn't know, but it seemed fitting for what she wanted. Beyond its open door, an ancient leather curtain sealed it from the glaring street. She pushed her way in. All the light in the church—and some unwanted warmth—came from candles arranged in stands before certain statues. Brigine looked around with a kind of desperate curiosity—she was not a Catholic. The church was empty but for one other person, a young woman lighting a candle before a statue of the Virgin. Silver hearts inscribed with thanks hung on the wall nearby. In a few moments she hurried out. Brigine took her place.

She put the book on the ground, and pushed it nearer the statue with her foot. She took two candles, lit them, and with trembling hands stuck them onto holders. She put the price of one candle only in the box. She whispered: "Please—will you take the book?"

The curtain moved, the air stirred, and gently every flame on the stand guttered out.

Weeks, months passed. She was having breakfast in a room with a view out over Sydney Harbor when she saw the headline: "Aurelia Sinks. Many Feared Lost." The Aurelia? *The Aurelia!* Reinhardt was on that ship, going to America. She knew because he had had to buy his tickets so long in advance. She jumped out of bed and grabbed the book. She started to write. The pen ran dry. She found a pencil—the lead broke. Oh, what could she use? She seized a lipstick. Well, why not? What did she care for the book now? She slashed his name onto the page:

Keep Reinhardt Mueller safe and well.

The letters looked like blood.

A curious feeling of warmth suffused her and a tremor passed

111

through the room like the first shiftings of an earthquake. At the same time the book—what was happening to the book! The pages started curling at the edges and a stench of charring leather rose nastily into the air. Then the door slammed back, and *he* stood there, dark once more—the chap with the eyebrows and the patent leather hair. "Fool!" he shrieked. "You can only ask for yourself! You're destroying the book!"

"I don't care."

A second tremor rattled the china and shook a picture from the wall. The devil—for it was a devil—blinked and calmed himself. "You've made a mistake. I know, *you want to save him for yourself.*"

"No."

"But you can have him back. Write it! Write it in the book."

"No."

Chairs fell over and the curtains billowed. The whole room started to vibrate. Flowers shed their petals and clothes flew out of the wardrobe.

Brigine tottered a little but she felt calm, as calm as in the gardens of the Villa Wurtz. And her heart grew lighter and lighter. A music stand crashed to the ground.

"What about your career?"

Her career! She held firm. "I'll risk it!"

"You can get to the top. You're not there yet, not quite."

She gathered herself and fought back: "I've done enough practice for ten violinists. Keep your rotten book. I'll manage on my own."

The room grew still, and very hot. It throbbed with heat. A great gout of flame leaped out of the book, and from its pages there arose a wailing. On every page—scorched and frail— Brigine could see long lists of names.

The devil was breathing strange shuddering breaths, and his limbs jerked. The pages crumpled, collapsed, and turned to ash.

Night and day flickered through the room, then Time ceased, and the book shriveled away—to nothing.

Brigine opened her eyes. She was alone. Her room was cool and orderly. She opened a window. The sea shone, white birds flew about, and the harbor fussed and teemed with life.

They haven't met since, but Reinhardt was saved. Brigine Damant still plays of course—I don't know if you've ever heard of her? She's a marvelous violinist.

As for black books—you take care, at sales and fairs and so forth. There's no reason to suppose that was the only one. . . .

The Parrot

BY VIVIEN ALCOCK

IT WAS ONE OF THOSE HAZY OCTOBER MORNINGS, WHEN THE weather may do anything, and you don't know what to wear. When I was halfway down Sebastian Street, the sun came out. I was too hot in my jacket, but couldn't be bothered to take it off. I already had enough to carry with my schoolbooks.

I don't know what made me look up. I don't often look up when I'm walking. I either look around to see if there's someone I know, or at the pavement before my feet, in case anyone has dropped some money.

I wasn't thinking of anything in particular. I can't remember hearing any odd sound. But something made me look up, sharply —and there it was. A gray, hunched bird, sitting in a tree, just above the high stone wall. It looked wet. Mist seemed to cling about it; and drops of water, like glass berries, hung on the branch beneath its claws. It looked as if it had been out in the rain all night, or maybe fallen into a bucket of water. The sunlight avoided it, as if it were a shadow.

114

It was a gray parrot, old, bedraggled, a most wretched bird. Even the rosy feathers on its tail looked cold, like a red nose in a winter face. Its eye was round, rain-colored, and fixed on me with a gloomy stare. As I stopped, it came hopping along the branch toward me, putting its head on one side in an anxious, ingratiating way, as if it wanted comfort, a friendly hand. . . .

Not my hand. I wasn't going to touch it. I stood, with my fists in my pockets and my heart banging loose in my chest. In spite of the sunlight and my new jacket, I began to shiver.

You'll think I was stupid to be scared of a parrot. All right! you'll say, maybe it *is* unusual to see a parrot loose in an English autumn when the nights are cold, but that's no reason to shake in your shoes like a thief. But you see, for a moment, I thought I knew that parrot. Only it wasn't possible! The parrot I had known must be dead. Dead and stiff on some lonely Devon hill.

When I was small, we lived in Devon, next door to a very old lady who had a parrot, a gray parrot with a rosy tail. Polly, she called him. Every year she went to visit her sister for a week, and as her sister did not like parrots, she asked my parents if we could look after him. In return, she offered to look after our cat, three gerbils, one hamster and a moth-eaten goldfish, when we went on holiday. If this seems an unequal bargain, with us getting the better part, then all I can say is—you didn't know that parrot.

He shrieked all day, a harsh, strange cry that frightened our cat and set our teeth on edge. He screamed as I sat puzzling over my sums, so that I could not hear myself count. He woke Bobby in his crib, drowned out the TV, made the neighbors complain. And if we put the cloth over his cage to silence him, we would sit there feeling guilty, thinking of the bird cramped in his unnatural night.

"Poor thing. He seems very unhappy," my mother said. "He's

probably missing Miss Brown. I expect he will settle down in a day or two."

After three days, he was quieter. I think he had screamed himself hoarse. There would be hours when he was silent, sitting hunched up in his gray wings, like an invalid in a shawl. I felt sorry for him. I came up to his cage, and he sidled along his perch to meet me, putting his head on one side and fixing me with his pearl-button eye.

"Pretty Polly. Pretty Polly," he said hopefully, and ducked his head down as if he wanted to be stroked. I put my finger through the bars of his cage . . . Crack! That iron beak had got it! I still have the scar. I'm lucky, I suppose, to have kept the finger that goes with it.

After that, we could not like Polly. We were kind to him, feeding him well, giving him the titbits he loved, grapes and pieces of banana; and keeping his cage clean. But we never liked him. And when the old lady died, and her sister came to her house to clear up, *she* did not want the parrot either.

She came smiling over the fence when Bobby and I were playing in the garden, and said, "I know my sister would have liked you to have Polly."

We looked at each other. Bobby put his finger in his mouth and his chin began to wobble. I said, "Oh, thank you, but— we've already got a lot of pets. Too many, Mom says. I don't think she'd let us have a parrot."

"I'm sure if you ask her nicely, she will. After all, you and Polly are old friends, aren't you? He'll feel quite at home."

We did not want Polly to feel at home in our house. We were frightened of him. But we were small, then, and shy of grown-ups; so when she said, "Run along and ask her, dears"—we went.

My mother was in the kitchen.

"She wants us to have old Miss Brown's Polly," I said.

" '*She*' is the cat's mother. If you mean Mrs. Jenkins, say so," said my mother improvingly. Then she took in what I had said. "No! Not that bird! Not ever again. I'm sorry, Anna, but that's final, so it's no use nagging and whining. . . ."

"I'll tell her," I said.

My mother looked surprised, not having expected such an easy victory. Not knowing we were on her side.

We ran back into the garden.

"Sorry. Mom says we can't have him," we said, trying to hide our relief.

"I don't know what to do," said Mrs. Jenkins, "I can't have him in my apartment. Pets are not allowed. He'll have to be put down."

As she said this, she looked at us slyly. Knowing children have kind hearts, she thought this would be enough to move us.

It did. It moved us to shame and guilt, so that when my father came home, I said, "Dad, Polly's going to be put down if we don't have him."

"Don't you believe it," said my father, "She's just trying it on. I'm not having a caged bird as a pet. It's cruel to keep them confined. There ought to be a law against it. Birds need to fly."

"I'll tell her myself in the morning that we can't have him." said my mother, "It's not as if she'll have any difficulty getting rid of him. She could always sell him to the pet shop. Parrots fetch quite a lot of money."

But in the morning, Bobby had a sore throat and spots, and Mom had to wait in for the doctor. So I went around to Mrs. Jenkins. Nobody had asked me to, but I was still young enough to like running errands; it made me feel important. Like a little parrot, I repeated what my father had said, that it was cruel to keep birds in cages. She looked offended. I told her my mother had said she could sell it for a lot of money. Now she looked interested. Then I spoiled it. "At least five pounds!" I invented, hoping to impress her. Five pounds was my idea of a fortune then.

It wasn't hers. I often wish I hadn't said that. Perhaps if she'd known how much parrots were really worth, she might have tried to sell him and things would have been different. . . .

"You won't have poor Polly put down, will you?" I said, "Promise?"

I suppose she kept her promise—in a way. That afternoon, when I was at school, she took his cage out into the garden and set him free. Mrs. King, who lived on the other side, watched from a bedroom window, and told us about it later. The parrot kept flying at the windows, trying to get in, she said, but Mrs. Jenkins had shut them all and put his cage in the garden shed. And when he perched in the apple tree, she came out with a broom and shooed him away, until at last he flew off into the huge, empty sky. I suppose she meant to be kind. But it was October then, as it is now, and although the sun was shining, the nights were cold.

My father was furious when he learned what she had done. I heard him talk to my mother about it; they did not know I was listening behind the door. The woman was a fool, he said. It would have been far kinder to have had the poor bird put to sleep. It had no chance of surviving the coming winter. No chance at all.

I cried that night, lying awake and warm beneath my blankets, thinking of the poor, cold bird flying over the dark, windy hills, trying in vain to escape the winter. And I felt guilty, knowing I had not begged and pleaded and whined for him, as I might have done for a new doll.

So you see now why I was startled—oh, to tell the truth, frightened—to see a gray parrot, sitting there like a ghost out of my past, staring at me with eyes as cold and pale as winter. But I was older now and sensible, though I say it myself. I knew it could not really be Polly. He could not have survived the bitter frosts of six long winters, nor flown two hundred miles to find us here in our London suburbs. There were other parrots, after all. The big pet shop in Camden Town sells blue macaws, white cockatoos, all sorts of parrots. Regents Park Zoo is not far away. Some other parrot must have escaped its cage.

I ought to tell someone, I thought. It'll die if it's not caught; the nights are cold now. I hesitated. I would be late for school if I didn't hurry. But I couldn't help that. I didn't want *this* parrot on my conscience.

I went back to the nearest house and knocked on the door. At first, no one came. I knocked again. A woman appeared, still in her dressing-gown. I could hear a baby crying in the house behind her. What did I want? A parrot in her garden? She knew nothing about it and cared less. "Try the corner shop," she suggested, as she shut the door, "They know everyone."

I thought this was a good idea. I knew the woman there; it was where I bought my candy. She was kind and liked animals. I started walking quickly, glancing up as I came to the tree on which the parrot had been sitting. It was still there.

"Don't worry," I said foolishly, "I'm getting help."

Then it spoke. Its voice was harsh, grating, as if its tongue were made of iron that had begun to rust.

"Go back!" it said, "Go back! Go back!"

I stopped—tried to go on but could not. I told myself that parrots only copy the noise words make. It was not really talking to me. But there was something so urgent, so foreboding in its voice, something so horribly familiar about its pale, sad eye, that I felt as if one of its scaly claws had clutched my heart. I thought —oh, it's stupid, I know—but I really thought it was Polly come back, out of his grave.

"What—P-Polly, is it you?" I stammered.

"Go back!" it said again, "Go back! Go back!"

I looked around. There was no one in sight. A car passed, but its windows were steamed up. I could not see the driver. The way

119

I felt at that moment, there might not have been one. Everything seemed strange. The sunlight fell coldly on the pavement, throwing shadows, sharp as knives. The leaves on the tree seemed to rattle together, as if they were fighting, pushing each other off the twigs into the gutter below. Winter was coming. I felt I could hear its heavy tread.

"I'm sorry, Polly," I said. "Honest, I cried when I heard what that horrid woman had done. I didn't want you to die. I couldn't have known, could I?"

I looked at it pleadingly, but all it said was "Go back! Go back! Go back!"

Was it warning me? Would something terrible happen if I went on? Its eye seemed transparent as glass, and yet . . . I had never known what it thought of me. It did not wag its tail like a dog, or purr like a cat when it was pleased. True, it had bitten my fingers once, which did not look like affection; but perhaps it had thought it was food, some small pink banana it was being offered for its tea? Perhaps the poor feathered ghost, for ghost I thought it was, was sorry it had hurt me and was trying to make amends by saving me from some horrible fate.

Or did it hate me? Had it always hated me for not loving it, blamed me for its sad end? Was it sending me back to be run over as I crossed the road, was a bomb going to blow up in the mail box as I crossed, or a slate fall off the roof onto my head? You see the fix I was in?

I dithered on the paving stone like someone on a shrinking island, unable to decide which way to escape. The sense of doom was so strong. To remain where I was might not be safe. Even now a thunderbolt might be descending on my head. I looked up hastily, but the sky was empty, a dead, colorless sky like the parrot's eyes.

"Go back!" the bird shrieked insistently. "Go back! Go back!"

Back where? My mother was at home. It was the thought of

her, plump and warm and smiling, that decided me. I started running back down the road, hearing behind me a harsh shriek and a flapping of gray wings.

I was careful, even then, frightened as I was. I looked both ways before I crossed the road. I made a wide circle around the mailbox. I raced down the path to our kitchen door so fast that no falling slate had a chance to hit me. The door was unlocked. I pushed it open so hard that it banged against the wall. Then I heard a great crash upstairs that set the teacups dancing on the dresser. And my mother screamed.

I have never run upstairs so fast. She was in Bobby's room, lying on the floor beside a fallen stepladder. And there was scarlet everywhere, on her dress, on the carpet . . . so much that I thought at first it must be paint. Then I saw her hand was clasping her arm, with blood pumping up between the fingers . . .

Her voice was faint. I had to bend down to hear it.

"Quick! Get Mrs. Jessop!" she said.

They told me later I *was* quick. They said I must have flashed next door like lightning. Dad says I'm a heroine, and Mom might have bled to death but for me. She had been changing a light bulb and had fallen off the ladder onto the glass lampshade, which she had thoughtlessly left lying on the floor. Mrs. Jessop, who had been to First Aid classes all last winter, had known what to do, and did it; while I dialed 999. It was something I had longed to do, but I was too upset to enjoy it.

After the ambulance had taken Mom to hospital, I told Mrs. Jessop about the parrot. Oh, not that I thought it was a ghost, just that I had seen one loose. She said, "Poor thing," but she was too full of what had happened to take much notice.

"Wasn't it lucky I took those First Aid classes!" she kept saying.

All that evening, Bobby and I went up and down the street, knocking on doors. But no one had seen a parrot. No one knew anyone who might have lost one. Nobody claimed it. We went to the police station and told the desk sergeant, and he promised they would look out for it.

"I shouldn't worry," he said. "Parrots are clever birds. When it feels cold, it'll soon find its own way home."

Perhaps it did. I never saw it again.

I've often thought about that parrot. I don't believe in ghosts. I'm twelve now and quite sensible. At least most of the time. I know it must have been some other parrot. London is a big place, and you don't always know the people living a street or two away. I like to think it belongs to an old lady, who loves it, and lets it fly about the gardens on sunny days. I can almost hear her, when the parrot returns, shooing it gently toward its open cage, calling out, "Go back! Go back! Go back!"

It is only sometimes, when winter is coming and the night are cold, that I wonder . . . When my mother came back from hospital, with seven stitches in her arm and a huge bandage, I asked her:

"What made you fall off the ladder?"

"I don't know, darling," she said, "Just carelessness, I expect."

"It couldn't have been a sudden noise, startling you?"

"A noise? No, I can't remember. What sort of noise?"

The noise of the kitchen door banging against the wall, when she thought she was alone in the house; the noise of my unexpected return. I think this, but I don't say it aloud.

So you see, if it was Polly come back, I still don't know what he intended. I like to think he was being kind, to make up for my bitten finger, and has now flown off happily to some bright jungle in the sky. But I can't be sure. What do you think?

Just a Guess

BY DICK KING-SMITH

THE FIRST THING YOU NOTICED ABOUT JOE WAS THE COLOR of his eyes. The table where Philip sat was close to Miss Atkinson's desk, and that morning she brought Joe into the classroom with her and stood him by her while she sat down and got out her register. All the children, boys and girls alike, were staring at the newcomer, some directly, some in a sideways fashion. There were some grins, a giggle or two. Joe looked around the room, and his eyes, Philip noticed, were a brilliant green. Cat's eyes. The bell rang.

"Good morning, children," said Miss Atkinson.

"Good morning, Miss Atkinson. Good morning all."

"Answer your names, please."

Reading the register took long enough for everyone to have a good look at Joe. He was tallish, thinnish, and his clothes were not very tidy. His face was very brown, his hair dark, long, a bit greasy. He did not seem embarrassed.

"Now, children," said Miss Atkinson, "as you can see, Top

123

Class has grown by one this morning. This is Joe Sharp. His family has just come to stay—that is, to live—in the village. Quite a large family too, I believe. You're the youngest, aren't you, Joe?"

"Yes, miss."

"And how many brothers and sisters have you?"

"No sisters, miss. Just six brothers."

"A seventh son, are you?" said Miss Atkinson, looking up.

I wonder, she thought, is it possible, could he be the seventh son of a. . . .

"Yes, miss," said Joe. "My father is too."

"Oh," said Miss Atkinson. "Yes. Well, now then, let me see." She looked around the class. "Philip. Philip Edwards. You're a sensible person. I want you to look after Joe if you will, please. Everything will be strange for him at first. Show him where everything lives. All right?"

"Yes, Miss Atkinson," Philip said. He saw the green eyes looking at him, and suddenly, for an instant, they shut, both together, in a kind of double wink.

"Now, Joe," said Miss Atkinson. "You sit next to Philip, there's room for you there, and I'll get you some exercise books. The rest of you, look at the blackboard, please, and get on with the work I've put up there. Later on this morning we have an interesting visitor coming in to school to talk to you. I'll tell you—no, I don't think I will. We'll leave it as a surprise."

She got up and went to the big stock cupboard at the far side of the room.

"Interesting visitor!" whispered Philip across the table.

"Hope it's Kenny Dalglish!"

"Kevin Keegan," whispered a boy opposite. "Kenny Dalglish is rubbish!"

"Football!" sneered a girl, wrinkling her nose.

"Copper," said Joe very quietly.

"What?"

"It'll be a copper."

"How do *you* know?"

"Just a guess."

"Shhh."

Miss Atkinson came back with a handful of books, a pencil, a ruler, an eraser.

When the bell went for morning playtime Philip said to the new boy, "Come on then. You'd better come with me. Better put your coat on, it's cold."

"I haven't got one," said Joe.

"Oh," said Philip. He put on his new jacket, blue with a red stripe down each arm and a furry hood. He felt a little awkward. "Birthday present," he said.

"November the twenty-third," said Joe.

"What?" said Philip in amazement.

"Just a guess."

"How . . . oh, I get it," said Philip. "You looked at the register. While Miss Atkinson was talking. You must have sharp eyes."

"Yes," said Joe.

In the roaring, screaming, galloping playground the two boys stood in a sheltered corner. Philip didn't feel he could dash off to play Bulldog with his particular friends, and the December winds were cold for someone without a top coat, especially somebody as thin as this one. He took a candy bar out of his jacket pocket.

"Have a bit?" he said.

"No thanks," said Joe. "Don't want to spoil my appetite for lunch. It's my favorite."

"What is?"

"Spam fritters and french fries."

Clever Dick, thought Philip, I've got him this time. He hasn't seen the list in the hall. He's just a know-it-all. It's roast beef.

125

"Want to bet?" he said.

"I haven't any money," Joe said.

"Well, I'll tell you what," Philip said. He put his hand in his trouser pocket. "I've got this ten-pence piece, see? If it is Spam fritters and french fries for lunch, I'll give it to you, just give it to you. If you're wrong, well, you needn't give me anything." That's fair, he thought. After all I do actually *know* it's roast beef.

"All right," said Joe. The green eyes looked straight into Philip's and then shut suddenly, momentarily, in that curious double wink. Philip wanted to smile back, but he felt embarrassed and began to flip the ten-pence piece in the air, using the pressure of thumb against forefinger, the proper way, the way referees did. He had only lately learned to do this and was proud of it.

Joe stood by him silently, shivering a little in the cold wind. A gang of younger boys dashed past, and one shouted "Who's your friend then, Phil?" A group of small girls in woolly hats cantered by, driving each other in harnesses made of skipping ropes. The horses neighed and the drivers cried "Gee up!" and "Steady!"

"Heads," said Joe suddenly. Philip, who had been catching the coin on the back of his left hand and covering it with the fingers of his right, exposed the result of the latest toss. It was a head.

"Try again," Philip said. He tossed the coin three times and each time Joe called correctly.

"You couldn't get it right ten times running," said Philip, "I bet you couldn't. Want to bet?"

"I haven't got any money," Joe said.

"Oh, it doesn't matter. Just try it."

Philip tossed his ten-pence piece ten times. Each time Joe called correctly. Philip scratched his head.

"How d'you do that?" he said.

"Just a guess."

"You're just lucky, I reckon. Let's try it again."

"No time," Joe said. "It's twenty to eleven. The bell will go any second."

Philip looked at Joe's thin bare wrists.

"How do you know?" he said. "You haven't got a watch."

The bell rang.

As they joined the rush back into school, Philip remembered what Miss Atkinson had said about an interesting visitor. What had Joe said? "Copper." I shouldn't be surprised, Philip found himself thinking, and then a funny shiver ran down his spine as they entered the classroom. The curtains were drawn, a screen was set up against one wall, and cables snaked across the floor to a film projector on Miss Atkinson's desk. She stood behind it, and beside her was the uniformed figure of a tall police sergeant.

"Sit down quietly, children," said Miss Atkinson. Philip forced himself not to look at his neighbor. He didn't want to see that double wink. His mind felt swimmy. Dimly he heard snatches of talk . . . "Sergeant Harrison . . . Road Safety Division . . . film to show you. . . ." and then a deep voice asking questions: "How . . . When . . . What would you do. . . . ?"

Hands were shooting up everywhere, and once he was conscious of Joe's voice answering something.

"Good. Very good indeed," said the sergeant. "I didn't expect anyone to know that one. How did you know, son?"

"Just a guess."

Then the projector began to run. It was a good film, an interesting film designed to catch and hold children's attention, and gradually Philip began to concentrate on it. It ended with a simulated road accident, where a boy dashed suddenly across a road, right under the wheels of a double-decker bus. It was very realistic.

The projector fell silent, and the only noise in the classroom was a thin metallic ssswish as Miss Atkinson opened the curtains. The sun had come out, and the audience blinked at the sudden light.

"One last thing," said Sergeant Harrison in his deep voice.

"One last piece of advice I've got for you. You've proved to me this morning that you know quite a bit about the Green Cross Code. You've answered most of my questions pretty well." He looked at Joe. "One of them very well. I shouldn't have expected any local lad to have been able to answer that particular one."

"Joe's new, Sergeant," said Miss Atkinson. "It's his first day. His people are travelers—you may have seen their caravans on the common. I expect he's been all over the place, have you, Joe?"

"Yes, miss."

"Ah, gypsy are you?" said Sergeant Harrison, but he did not say it unkindly, and he smiled as he said it.

"Yes, sir."

"Reckon you'll be here long?"

"No, sir."

Philip felt a sudden ache.

"Anyway," said the sergeant. "As I was saying. Here's one last piece of advice. You all saw how that film finished. Well, don't . . . think . . . it . . . can't . . . happen . . . to . . . you. We all know that was only a mock-up. The boy acting the part didn't get killed, of course. But boys do, and girls, somewhere, every day of every week of every year. So don't think 'that couldn't be me.' It could. So take care."

"Paint monitors," said Miss Atkinson a quarter of an hour later, when the screen and projector had been stowed away, and the tall sergeant had put on his peaked cap and gone. "Angela. Sue. Judith. Would you please put the tables ready after you've had your lunch. That film should have left us all with lots of pictures in our minds. This afternoon we'll see if we can put them on paper. Now go and wash your hands, everybody, and line up by the hall door."

Standing beside Joe in the line, Philip listened to the pair in front.

"What is it today?"

"Roast beef."

"Ugh!"

"Don't you like it?"

"Not much."

They all trooped in, and when places had been settled and grace said, Mrs. Wood, the cook, appeared in the doorway of the kitchen.

"I'm sorry, children," she said, "there's been a bit of a mixup. The beef for today's lunch didn't turn up, but I don't think you'll be too disappointed." She paused.

Philip put his hand in his pocket.

"It's Spam fritters and french fries," she said.

There were one or two "oh's," a loud murmur of "*mmm!s.*"

"Quiet, please," said the teacher on dinner duty.

"Keep it," whispered Joe. "You keep it." Philip took his hand out of his pocket. He looked at Joe and got the double wink.

After lunch, in the playground, everybody knew. Top Class had told the rest, and somehow everyone except the littlest ones managed to pass close to the spot where Philip and Joe were standing. A gypsy! There was giggling. Philip could hear some of the passing comments and they were not kind. "My dad says they're dirty." "They steal things." "Horses." "Babies." More giggles. "They eat hedgehogs." A snort of laughter.

"Can you tell fortunes, diddakoi?' said Mickey Bean, a big boy who was always looking for trouble and finding it. He stood in front of Joe, quite close, picking his nose with his thumb. Philip felt himself grow suddenly, furiously, angry.

"I can, Mickey," he said in a choky voice, "and yours is, you'll get your face smashed in."

Mickey Bean took his thumb out and clenched his fist.

"Why, you . . ." he began, but Joe said quietly "Pack it in." He looked at Mickey with his green eyes, and after a moment Mickey looked away.

"Come on, Phil," said Joe, and they walked off together.

"That was nice of you," he added, "sticking up for me."

They stood side by side at the far end of the playground, their fingers hooked through the wire mesh of the boundary fence, and stared at the traffic going up and down the village street. Philip swallowed.

"Can you?" he said. "Tell fortunes, I mean?"

"Fortunes?" Joe said. "I dunno about fortunes. I know what's going to happen. Sometimes. Not always of course."

"Well, could you . . ." Philip looked around, "could you . . . tell what will be the next thing to come around the corner, down there, at the end of the street?"

"Probably," Joe said. "Want to bet?" he said, and he gave the double wink, very quickly. The twinkling of an eye, two eyes rather, thought Philip, grinning.

"I haven't got any money," he said. "What's in my pocket is yours, really."

"Well, all right then, if I'm wrong," said Joe, "it's your again."

"O.K.," Philip said. They stared down the street, empty for a moment.

"Private car," Joe said. " 'S' Registration. 4-door. Pale blue. Lady driving." He paused. "It's a Ford."

They waited five, ten seconds. Suddenly a car came around the wall of the end house in the street, and drove up toward them, and passed them. It was a 4-door "S" Registration sedan with a lady at the wheel. It was pale blue.

"It's a Vauxhall," Philip said slowly. He looked sideways at Joe.

"Just a guess," Joe said. "You have a go," he said.

Philip tried "Red car" and got a bicycle; "Lorry" and got the mail truck; "Bus" and around the corner came an old Morris 1000. "It's Miss Atkinson," he said as it drew near and began to indicate a turn into the school road. "I expect she's been down to Beezer's. She often goes at lunchtime." Beezer's was the village shop which sold everything you could imagine, and Philip was about to explain this to the new boy when it occurred to him that he needn't bother. Joe probably knew exactly what she'd bought. Before he could voice the thought, Joe said, "All right, if you really want to know—a small brown loaf, six oranges, and a box of soap. Oh, and something wrapped in newspaper. Not sure what it is. It's dirty, I think."

And of course when Miss Atkinson had disappeared into the school, and they wandered down and peeped in the car, there they were on the back seat—bread, fruit, soap powder, and a head of celery.

Philip's earlier feeling about Joe, a scary feeling that the green eyes could somehow see into the future, had already altered quite a bit. It wasn't a feeling now, it was a certainty, and therefore not as frightening, though just as exciting.

"I suppose you know what I'm going to paint this afternoon," he said.

"Yes," Joe said.

At that moment the bell rang for afternoon school. The tables were ready, covered with old newspapers, the paints, brushes, palettes, and mixing dishes put out.

"Painting aprons, everybody, and sleeves rolled tightly, please," said Miss Atkinson. "Joe Sharp, I've got an old shirt for you from my odds-and-ends cupboard."

I know exactly what I'm going to paint, thought Philip. How curious that someone else does too. Before I've even made a mark on the paper.

He began to draw with a pencil, little figures, lots of them, like matchstick men. It was to be a picture of the children coming out of school and crossing the road. With Mrs. Maybury, the crossing guard. And lots of cars and buses and trucks and motorbikes. He was so absorbed that it was some time before he realized that Joe's paper was still quite blank.

"What's the matter, Joe?" said Miss Atkinson, coming around. "Aren't you feeling well?"

"Too many Spam fritters," someone said, and there was giggling.

"I'm all right, miss," Joe said softly.

"Well, come along then. You must make a start. Think about this morning's film. Haven't you got some sort of picture in your mind?"

"Yes, miss," Joe said. He picked up a brush and began to put paint on his piece of paper, big splashes of it, with big brush strokes, very quickly. Miss Atkinson went away, and Philip began to color in his matchstick men, carefully, neatly. He forgot about Joe or indeed anybody else in the room until he heard Miss Atkinson's voice again.

"Why, Joe," she said, "that's a strange picture. What's it supposed to be?"

"It's an accident, miss," Joe said, and Philip, turning to look, found the green eyes fixed on him with the strangest expression. Quickly Philip looked at Joe's picture. There were no figures in it, no shapes. There were just splodges of color on a background of bluey-black. At one side there was something that might have been a tree, or a post perhaps, with a stripey trunk bent over in the middle, an orange blob on the end of it. Under that there was a red squidge, and in the middle of the painting a kind of checkered path with a big dark mass on it.

"Yes," Miss Atkinson said. "I see."

"What is it?" Philip whispered when she had gone away. "What's the matter? Why are you looking at me like that?"

"It's nothing," Joe said, and then suddenly, violently, he jumped to his feet, knocking over his chair, and picking up his painting he tore it noisily across, in half, then into quarters, and then again and again till there wasn't a piece bigger than a postage stamp. Everyone stared open-mouthed.

"Joe!" cried Miss Atkinson. "What in the world . . . ? Look, young man, I don't give out good quality paper and expensive paints so that you can. . . ." She stopped, seeing the curious pallor in the brown face. "Are you quite sure you're feeling all right?"

"Yes, miss. Sorry, miss," Joe said.

"Well, it's too late to start again now," Miss Atkinson said. "Put all those scraps into the wastepaper basket. The rest of you, finish off as soon as you can and start tidying up."

"Wait for me," Joe said, when they had been dismissed and were crossing the road with a crowd of others under Mrs. Maybury's eagle eye. It was raining and misty and getting dark all at once, and the water ran off the crossing guard's cap and yellow oilskins. There was only one sidewalk in this part of the street, so everybody crossed before turning their separate ways.

"We can walk down together," Philip said. "If your, um, caravan's on the common, I live down that way. Our house is called. . . ." "I know," said Joe. "Of course," Philip said.

"The only difference is," he went on, "that you can stay on this side now, but I cross over the crosswalk."

"Between Beezer's and the Post Office," Joe said.

"Yes."

"You *mustn't*."

133

"What?"

"You mustn't. Whatever you do, you mustn't go on that crosswalk crossing tonight."

"Oh, but look," Philip said, "I promised Mom I'd always use the crossing. The traffic whizzes along here. And you heard what the policeman said this morning about crosswalks."

"You mustn't," Joe said doggedly, the rain running down his hair and making it look longer and greasier than ever.

"It was that painting of yours, wasn't it?" said Philip. "You sort of saw something in it, did you?" Joe nodded.

"Yes, but after all that's just. . . ."

"Just a guess," Joe said.

Philip stopped and looked into the green eyes. They shut, quickly, in the double wink, and Philip grinned.

"Oh, all right," he said, "if it makes you any happier I'll cross over earlier."

They walked on a bit till they came opposite the post office, where there was a sidewalk on each side of the street. Philip looked left, looked right, looked left again, and went carefully over.

They walked on, on opposite sides now, till they came to the crosswalk, where they stopped and faced one another across the road. It was nearly dark, and the street lights made yellow reflections in the pools of water glistening on the road.

"G'night then, Joe," Philip called. "See you in the morning," but any answer was drowned in a sudden squealing of brakes. The red sports car, traveling fast, tried too suddenly to stop at the sight of two boys, both apparently about to cross. The tires found no grip on the wet surface and the car skidded wildly sideways, straight at Joe.

Philip heard a crash as it hit the signal light, which broke, almost in the middle, so that the top part with its orange ball came slowly down like a flag lowered to half mast.

134

"He guessed wrong! He guessed wrong! He guessed wrong!" went racing through Philip's brain. He had not seen Joe's wild leap to safety. The car obscured it, and the rain, and the gloom.

"Joe! Joe!" Philip shouted, and he ran madly across the crosswalk.

He did not see the truck, and the truck did not see him. Until the last moment.

Which was too late.

The Boy's Story

BY CATHERINE STORR

"TELL ME A STORY. A GHOST STORY," THE BOY SAID.

"I don't know any stories about ghosts," the father answered.

"Haven't you ever seen a ghost?" the boy asked.

"No."

"Hasn't anyone you've ever known seen a ghost?"

"No."

"How do you know? Someone might have seen a ghost and you didn't know about it."

"People I know don't see ghosts. They're not that sort," the father said.

"What sort of people see ghosts?" the boy pursued.

"I don't know. Weird people. Not anyone like you and me."

The boy sighed. Ordinary people, it seemed, like his father and himself, didn't see ghosts. Where, then, were the ghosts? Who saw them? Who wrote ghost stories? Only the weirdos? Where did they get their ideas from? He tried again.

"If you saw a ghost now, what would you do?"

"Here? In the middle of the town? In daylight?"

"It's not all that daylight now. But suppose you were all alone here in the middle of the night, and you saw a ghost. What would you do then?"

"How would I know it was a ghost?" the father asked. He was a practical man. Or so he always said.

"You'd know," the boy said, confident.

"I'd take no notice," the father said.

"Suppose it started coming after you?"

"If I wasn't taking any notice of it, I wouldn't know it was coming after me, would I?"

"You'd feel it coming. Not running. Slowly."

"Exactly where do I see this ghost?" the father asked, humoring his son.

The boy thought. He looked around the crowded street. He looked at the bright shop windows, sprinkled with imitation frost and dressed in sparkling silver and gold and scarlet, for Christmas. He looked at the massed cars, moving snail-pace along the crowded street, at the tall double-decker buses full of faces peering out through the steamed-up windows. He tried to imagine the place dark, silent and deserted. It was difficult, now that it was all cheerful bustle and glitter, the sidewalks thronged with other shoppers, carrying gaily wrapped packages and shouting to make themselves heard above the noise of gears changing and horns pooping. It would be another world.

Then he saw that some of the shops had entrances set back from the sidewalks. Just now these entrances were brilliant with light from the bright windows which flanked them. But he had imagination. He pointed.

"There. You see it standing there." He could almost see it himself. When the shop windows were darkened there would be shadows which the streetlights overhead wouldn't reach.

137

His father hadn't paid much attention to the pointing finger. "In the shop?" he said, and laughed.

"In the doorway. You don't notice it at first. Not until you're walking right past, like we are now. And then you see. No. You don't see. You walk almost past, and then you feel."

"Feel? What?"

"Just something. Cold."

"Cold?"

"And you look sort of sideways. Without moving your head, because you don't want it to think you're really looking. But you do see it. Just standing. It doesn't move. Not then."

"What does it look like? I suppose it's wearing armor. Has its head under its arm. Something like that?" the father said, willing to play along with the game.

"You don't see properly. Remember, it's dark. But it's partly because you're looking sideways, not straight at it. So you don't know exactly what it's like. You just have this feeling, that it's there because of you. Waiting for you."

"I'd walk past."

"You do walk past. But then you start wondering. Whether there really was anything there."

"I could always go back and have another look to make sure," the father said.

"You'd never do that!" the boy said.

"Why wouldn't I?"

"Because you're frightened. You don't want to go back. You want to get away as quickly as you can."

"Even though I'm not sure whether I saw anything or not?" the father asked.

"You hope you didn't, but really you know you did."

"So I walk away, like we're walking now?"

"Only it's not like this. It's all quiet. There aren't any other people, or cars or anything. There's only you. And it, of course."

138

"I could do without these crowds. Get on a bit faster," the boy's father said.

"That's what you'd like to think," the boy said.

"Why don't I, then?"

"Because you're listening all the time."

"Listening for what?"

"The footsteps."

"What do you mean, footsteps? If there aren't any other people."

"*Its* footsteps. What you hope you didn't see."

"Running after me?"

"Not running. Just walking, like you are. Not any faster, not catching up. You can't be sure you really hear them, because they're going the same pace as you, and if you stop, they stop too. You don't know if they're really there, or if it's just your own footsteps you're listening to."

"I'd turn around and have a look," the father said.

"No."

"Why not? That'd be the sensible thing to do."

"You aren't feeling sensible," the boy answered.

The father was tired of the game. He said, "Hungry? What about some tea? They have crumpets at Jerningham's. We have to go there anyway to get the gear your Mom wants for icing the cake."

They went through the swinging doors into the great lighted jostling store, the high ceiling garlanded with paper chains, tinsel and holly twisted around the staircase rails and up the imitation marble pillars. A gilded cage shot them up five floors to the restaurant, and, sitting high above the sparkling streets, they drank hot, sweet, brown tea, and sucked the salty butter out of crumpets with as many holes in their pale faces as a sponge. At last, pleasantly full, licking the salt from their lips, they went down in the lift to the basement. There they searched for and found the gadget needed by the boy's mother, then mounted an escalator, reached the ground floor and fought their way through the crowd to the doors leading out into the street. By now the street lamps were lit. The shop windows blazed with an extra radiance. Behind the plate glass an assortment of objects was displayed to tempt last-minute shoppers. But the boy hardly glanced at them. Most of them were grown-up things anyway. Who wanted to get a washing machine for a Christmas present? Or an armchair? It was stupid, too, to pretend that great big things like that could be wrapped in colored paper and tied up with ribbons like a box of chocolates. His legs ached, and the heat of the big store had made him sleepy. He wouldn't have minded going home. He pressed closer to his father's side.

"Where are we going now?" he asked.

"Got to get a bit of wood, fifty-four by ninety by five, for the shelf in the pantry. Half a dozen cup hooks and a tin of varnish. Might call in and see if Charlie at Deckers has got the beading I asked him for. That's all," the father said.

They walked further along the crowded street to the builders' merchant, where the piece of wood, fifty-four by ninety by five should have been waiting, ready cut for them. But they had to wait. In the Christmas rush it had been stacked somewhere out at the back, no one was sure where. The boy sat on a chair by the high counter and looked, without really seeing, at all the tools arranged in precise order of their uses and graded in size, making patterns in the display on the opposite wall. He fumbled in the shopping bag he held, and found the carton of peppermint drops which he'd bought earlier in the day. He unwrapped one and sucked it dreamily while he waited, thinking about nothing in particular, too tired even to be bored.

It was over an hour later when, the wood and the beading at last collected, the father and son began their return journey along the shopping street. And now everything had changed. The

140

shoppers were all gone. The place had an empty, lost look. Tatters of colored paper lollipop sticks and bus tickets littered the sidewalks. A slight, cold rain was falling. Just now there were no buses on the road, and only the occasional car, the red rear lights looking like the eyes of some wild animal backing away from them along the deserted street.

They passed Jerningham's, alive only an hour ago with busy shoppers. Now the gilded doors were firmly shut, and inside the dim lights showed no movement, only the shapes of sheeted stands and counters, a shadowy emporium served by nothing but a skeleton staff. The man and the boy walked on, past more closed doors and windows, in which the lights were being, one by one, extinguished. They walked slowly, the man encumbered by the piece of wood under his arm and the parcels which dangled from his hand. The boy was tired; they had been out for a long time. He lagged behind, and his father called to him sharply.

"Get a move on, son. We don't want to take all day, do we?"

"I'm coming as fast as I can," the boy said.

"Come on, then."

As the father turned back to make for the bus station around the next corner, his glance fell across the window of the shop they were passing. In that split second he had the curious impression that a pair of eyes were regarding him steadily from behind the glass. Huge, dark eyes, as large as the eye sockets in a. . . . He turned quickly to look more carefully, and saw that what he had mistaken for the fixed, sightless stare of a skull was nothing but a pair of spectacles, suspended halfway up the window by a thread which he hadn't seen in this half light. Reassured, he turned back once more, and by this time his stride, which had hardly faltered, had carried him past the window. Now he was level with the entrance to the shop itself, one of those deep entrances, the door sat ten feet or so back from the pavement and flanked by the shrouded sides of the two windows. Somehow it seemed familiar, and at first he couldn't think why. Then he remembered. It was an entrance like this to which the boy had pointed, hours ago, during that silly conversation about ghosts. It could even have been this very one; he hadn't taken that much notice. But the memory was an uncomfortable one, and he felt a tiny shiver run down his spine. But that was ridiculous. Of course there would be nothing in the doorway that shouldn't be there, even where the shadows were blackest. Yet he felt an uneasy reluctance to turn his head and to look directly in. Of course if he did, he would see that there was nothing there. But to feel obliged to look was silly . . . childish. He really did not mean to look. But in spite of himself, his eyes slewed round just as he reached the further side of the entrance, his sight trying to penetrate that patch of densest darkness at the far end of the short passageway.

What happened next had nothing to do with his thinking self. It was the impulse of blind panic. Before he knew what he was doing, he had clutched the boy's wrist with his free hand, and he was running down the empty street, the unwieldy length of wood biting into his side, the parcels hanging from his wrist swinging against his thigh. His breath came in short, painful gasps, the fierce beating of his heart hammered in his ears. He felt deafened by its insistent pounding and yet through everything he could hear footsteps behind him. Not the lighter steps of his son, dragging at his hand, but heavier steps, measured with his own, echoing from the deserted pavement and from the blank, dead windows of the shuttered shops.

He checked himself at last at the corner of the big road, busy with cars, and with people pushing toward the bus station and the car park. Less than twenty yards away he could see the familiar shape of the red bus waiting for them, full of light and passengers. Many passengers, he was reassured to notice. He slowed to walking pace. He needed to recover his dignity. He shifted the awkward length of timber under his arm, released the boy's wrist and changed the hanging parcels to the other hand.

"Thought we were going to miss the bus," he said.

"You hurt me. You almost pulled my arm out of its socket," the boy complained as they joined the line.

"Thought we were late," the man said.

"There's another bus goes at seven. We could have got that," the boy said. Then looking down, he said, reproachful, "I've dropped my candy. You made me drop my candy. They were on top of my shopping bag, and now they're not there. They must've fallen out when you made me run like that."

"Never mind. They don't matter," his father said.

"I do mind. They cost thirty pence," the boy said.

"I'll give you the thirty pence," his father said.

"But it's a waste. We could go back and look for them. There's plenty of time. . . ."

"We're not going back," the man said. He was shouting. The boy looked at him, surprised. The man said, more quietly, "No point in going back. We'd better get on the bus."

The boy followed his father, wondering, as he often did, at the way grown-up people behaved. Sometimes when you thought everything was all right, they got cross. Sometimes they laughed at what you said, when there wasn't anything funny about it. Now Dad shouted at him for nothing. You'd have thought he'd be pleased to save thirty pence instead of getting het up at the idea of going back to look for the box of candy. He saw his father stow the length of wood and the larger parcels in the baggage space. The boy pushed into the window side of the seat. The man sat beside him, thankful for the chance to sit down in the light and in company. His legs were trembling—from the unaccustomed exercise, of course.

The bus ground its gears, inched out into the road and lum-

143

bered off away from the lighted streets of the town. Soon it was lurching along the unlit country roads, where the blackness was broken here and there by the yellow lights of cottage windows, and where giant skeleton trees loomed suddenly, scratching the windows of the upper deck with bony fingers, as if they might break through the glass and snatch the faces inside to carry them off to the sightless world without. The boy leaned against his father, going over in his mind the events of the afternoon. He thought of the presents he'd bought for his brother and small sister, of the handkerchief he'd got for Mother. He thought of the sweet rubbery flesh of the crumpets and of the soppy music they'd listened to while they ate their tea. He thought of the shops they'd passed earlier, while they were still brightly lit and he'd picked out things he'd have liked for himself in their windows. He thought of the conversation he'd had with his father there.

He said, drowsily, "What would you really do if you saw a ghost, Dad?" It didn't surprise him that, in the usual grown-up way, his father didn't answer that properly. Instead he said, "We had to catch this bus. Mom would have worried. She might have thought something had happened to us."

The boy said, "No, she wouldn't. She'd know we'd come back all right."

Some quality in his father's silence made him repeat, "She'd know we were all right. There isn't anything could happen to us. Could it, Dad?"

His father said, quickly, "Of course not. What could happen to us?"

Welcome, Yule

BY JAN MARK

PROBABLY EMMA WOULD NOT HAVE COME TO KNOW MR. Jarvis, the new vicar, if someone had not tipped him off that her dad could play the organ. They never discovered who had done it, although Dad did say that whoever it was ought to be hung up by the heels and skinned with a butter knife, which would have been worth watching, but one day the vicar arrived on his motorcycle, without warning. Emma came home from school and found him in the living room with a cup of tea at his elbow, Mom hovering and Dad cowering.

"I believe you're something of an organist," said the vicar to Emma's dad, who was off work with a broken finger. He was a draftsman as Featherstone's.

"Not at the moment," Dad said, waving his fat finger like a parsnip in its bandages.

"Well, that won't last forever," the vicar said.

"Nor will I," Dad said, glumly. He hated to be ill, even in one finger. Emma loved it because she was healthy and hardly ever had a day off from school.

"It would only be two weeks in three," said Mr. Jarvis. "There's no music at Holy Communion." He would not give in. After about an hour, Dad gave in, because his finger would keep him off the keys for at least another month and, as the vicar had said, it was only two Sundays out of three.

Ockney, Cawley and Strang shared one vicar among them. Emma lived in Strang, and the vicar did too, because it was the largest parish. It had municipal housing, a factory, and the smallest Woolworth's in England, perhaps in the whole world. On Sundays the vicar buzzed in a beeline from church to church on his motorcycle; Holy Communion at Ockney, Matins at Strang and Evensong at Cawley. On the following Sunday they each celebrated a different service. Emma thought it was like musical chairs, and wondered what would happen if one of the churches fell down during the week, and the vicar was left stranded with a spare service and nowhere to say it. Churches had fallen down before. On the hill above Strang, between Highmead Estate and Featherstone's Marine Diesel Engines Ltd, lay the remains of St. Thomas's church. Six hundred years ago old Strang village had stood on the hill around St. Thomas's, but after the great epidemic called the Black Death, which had wiped out all but seven parishioners, the village moved away and started again in the valley, with a new church, Holy Trinity, which showed no signs of falling down.

Up on the hill, St. Thomas's slid gently back into the ground until the grass covered it, and now the local children played on the green lumps and bumps that had been the nave and chancel. They preferred it to the town playground where there were swings and slides and concrete pipes to crawl through. Emma herself preferred it. She did not live in municipal housing, but she often went up to play at St. Thomas's.

146

"I'm not playing on some old church," said her cousin Naomi, when she came to stay. "It's spooky," Naomi said, before she had even seen it.

"It's not," Emma said.

"I bet there's ghosts."

"I've never seen one," Emma retorted. "Not up there, at any rate."

"Where then? Bet you never."

"Bet what you like. You wouldn't know a ghost if you saw one," Emma said, and they went off to play in the concrete pipes.

The vicar came to see Dad in July. By September Dad couldn't pretend any longer that his finger was stiff, so all through the autumn he went down to Holy Trinity, two weeks out of three, to play the organ at Matins or Evensong. Mother and Emma, who had never been churchgoers, sometimes went along too, to lend him moral support, and often Mr. Jarvis visited them to discuss next week's music. Dad found himself playing the organ at choir practices as well, at weddings and funerals, and then suddenly it was November, and the vicar began to talk about Christmas carols.

Winter had come early that year. The vicar stood on the frosty doorstep, staring at the black sky and the burning blue stars, while his breath steamed in the light from the hall, and the hall grew colder and colder. Mom and Emma huddled around the stove in the kitchen and wished that Dad were brave enough to boot the vicar out and shut the door. At last they heard the roar of his two-stroke as he shot away down the hill.

"One of these nights he'll come off at that bend by the bridge," Mom said, hopefully, as Dad came back into the hall and shut the door.

"He thinks there'll be snow before Christmas," Dad said, rushing to the stove with his purple hands held out in front of him, like a rocket-powered sleepwalker. "Says he can smell it."

147

"All right for some," Mom said. "They've got central heating at the vicarage."

"He wants to go carol singing," said Dad.

"I can just see that," said Mom. "I can just see him belting round the county on his Yamaha, singing 'Silent Night' fit to raise the dead."

"Not by himself," Dad said. "He thinks we should all go out with the three church choirs and tramp round Ockney and Cawley as well. Candle lanterns and mulled ale and Jack Pewsey with his clarinet."

"Jack plays hot jazz," Mom pointed out.

"I think we could cool him down enough for a few carols."

"The weather'll do that," Mom said.

"It had better. If it's not Jack Pewsey it'll be me with a portable harmonium and four Boy scouts to pull it."

"The Baptists at Ockney have a harmonium," said Mom. "It sounds like a string quartet in a drain."

"I know—I'll go down to the *Three Compasses* and buy Jack a few pints," said Dad.

Emma said, "If you go carol singing, can I come?"

"We'll all come," Mom said. She turned to Dad who was putting on his parka. "The vicar wasn't there last Christmas, was he?"

"Came just before Easter. I remember the first time I saw him —lurking under the lych-gate on Good Friday."

"Then someone ought to tell him about the Waits. He shouldn't upset the Waits."

The vicar's idea caught on. Everybody in Ockney, Cawley and Strang wanted to go out carol singing at Christmas, although not all of them wanted to go with the vicar. Strang Women's Institute decided to dress up in Olde Tyme clothes and go around with a sled, distributing tea and sugar to the Old Age Pensioners.

Cawley School got up a rival scheme involving Christmas puddings, while the Ockney Baptists wheeled out their portable harmonium and began rehearsing on their own account. On still evenings it could be heard even by the nightwatchman up at Featherstone's Marine Diesels. The vicar became concerned by the threat of so much competition and planned a campaign to eliminate it. He called a meeting in the parish room at Strang, to explain his strategy.

He had brought along a map of the three parishes, divided up into zones with red lines and arrows. Emma, looking at it, was reminded of a plan for battle. She could picture Mr. Jarvis lying in ambush with his carol singers armed and hidden behind a hedge, waiting for the Ockney Baptists to come wheezing by. The vicar explained what the red lines were for.

"Carol singing starts a week before Christmas. The W.I. are going round Cawley and Ockney on the twentieth and twenty-third, and Strang on the twenty-second. Cawley School will be in Ockney on the twenty-fist, Strang on the twenty-third, and at home on the twenty-second. Ockney Baptists will be in Strang on the twenty-first, and Ockney and Cawley on the twenty-second and twenty-third. How's that for dovetailing?" said the vicar.

"What about us?" Dad asked.

"Aha," the vicar said, teeth glistening with satisfaction. "The united church choirs will be at Ockney on the nineteenth, and Cawley on the twenty-first, but we'll be in Strang on the twentieth. That, you see—if you'll just look at this chart—gives us the first crack at Ockney and Strang. No one will have been round before us."

"And first crack at the collection," Dad muttered.

"What about the Waits?" Emma asked. She nudged Dad. "Mom told you to tell him about the Waits."

Dad looked embarrassed. "It's not that simple, Em."

Emma could believe it. The vicar was not the kind of man to listen to things that he did not want to hear, but she was firm. She prodded her father.

"Go on, Dad."

Dad coughed. "Er, Mr. Jarvis . . . is this absolutely final?" he asked, pointing to the map.

"And foolproof," said the vicar. "Why, is there a fly in the ointment? Trust you to find it."

"Not exactly. It's just that the Waits always sing in Strang on the twentieth. It's St. Thomas's Eve, you see. . . ."

"Waits? Of course I know it's St. Thomas's Eve. What Waits?"

"Waits. You know, the old name for carol singers," Dad said.

"Ah, yes; Middle English, from Old Norman French *waitier* from the Old French *guaitier* . . . What about them? We've not had any complaints from them?"

"Well, you wouldn't," Dad mumbled, "but they might not like it."

"Who are these Waits? A music society?"

"You could call them that," Dad agreed.

"If they wanted to book the twentieth, they should have spoken up. I announced the provisional dates ten days ago. No one said anything. Who's their chairman, or secretary, or whatever they have?"

"I don't think they have one," said Dad. "They're not an official society, just local people who like to come together to sing carols on St. Thomas's Eve. It's a kind of tradition," he said, lamely.

"They're perfectly welcome to join our band," the vicar declared, brisk and reasonable. "I'll say as much on Sunday."

On Sunday, at Evensong, he announced that the Waits would be very welcome to come carol singing with the united church choirs of Ockney, Cawley and Strang, on the twentieth of December, but not on any other night, and not on their own.

150

"We don't want clashes between rival supporters," the vicar said, with a jolly smile. There was an uneasy, almost angry, muttering among the congregation.

"I'll be very surprised," Mother said, under her breath, "if anyone from Strang turns out for His Nibs on the twentieth."

School ended on Tuesday the nineteenth, and that evening Mother and Dad and Emma wrapped up warmly, collected Jack Pewsey, who was Emma's headmaster, and Jack's clarinet, and drove over icy roads to Ockney, where they met the three choirs assembled outside the *King's Head*, and sang "O Come All Ye Faithful" by way of a warm-up, before moving on to render "The Holly and the Ivy"—with particular emphasis on the line about the playing of the merry organ, to the Baptists, practicing in the chapel with their harmonium.

Next day, on the morning of the twentieth, Jeck Pewsey rang up, in a hoarse voice, to say that the cold air had got to his lungs and he wouldn't be able to play his clarinet in Strang that night.

"Lungs, my foot," said Mom. "He doesn't want to upset the Waits, that's what."

"Sensible fellow," Dad said, and rang the vicar.

"I think we'll have to call it a day, tonight," he said, but the vicar rang up the Ockney Baptists and that afternoon the pastor drove over in his minibus and unloaded the portable harmonium at Emma's front gate, just as Dad was coming home from Featherstone's.

"But won't you need it yourselves?" Dad asked, with wan hope.

"Not till Thursday, thanks to Generalissimo Jarvis," the pastor said, leaping back into the minibus. He was an athletic man. He had unloaded the harmonium single-handed. It took the combined efforts of Mom, Dad and Emma to move it into the garage.

"No luck," Dad said. "I'll have to go through with it." He looked with loathing at the minibus, skidding around the bend

151

by the bridge. "Why do clergymen drive so badly? I knew this mad monk in Macclesfield—he had a Volvo. . . ."

"We'll come too," Emma said, firmly. If the Waits turned out for a showdown with the vicar, she wanted to be there to see it.

They gathered under a starry sky in frozen silence, by the west door of Holy Trinity. The choir from St. Mary's Ockney was there, and the choir of Cawley All Saints, but from Strang there was no one but Mom, Dad, Emma and the vicar.

"I see," said Mr. Jarvis, peering into the darkness. "I see."

"I doubt it," said Emma's dad, bold after a couple of whiskies with Jack Pewsey who had claimed that his tubes needed flushing and coughed hollowly to prove it. "The Waits sing tonight."

"And people in Strang prefer to go out with the Waits rather than support their own church choir?"

"No one goes out with the Waits," Dad said, "but it's their night, and no one wants to offend them."

"They had plenty of warning," the vicar snapped. He turned to the four Boy Scouts, harnessed like reindeer to the Baptists' harmonium. "One, two, three—*heave!*"

The choirs moved off, and did not halt until they reached the bridge where Emma's own road went around the corner.

"We'll begin with 'Once in Royal David's City,'" the vicar announced.

Dad unfolded his camp stool, sat down at the harmonium, and began to play. The choirs began to sing. After they had finished with Royal David's City the Scouts went round knocking on doors, while Dad struck up "Good King Wenceslas." It was a good carol for a cold night, and the choirs sang vigorously, but at the end of every verse Emma could have sworn that somewhere, not too distant, another choir was singing "Good King Wenceslas," four bars behind.

" 'O Little Town of Bethlehem,' " the vicar commanded when they had finished, and they began again. This time there could be no doubt. Somewhere in the streets of Strang, another choir was singing; *not* "O Little Town of Bethlehem." When "O Little Town of Bethlehem" was over, they all paused to listen. Across the frosty rooftops chimed the strains of a carol that Emma had never heard before, but rather liked:

> *Out of your sleep arise and wake,*
> *For God mankind now hath y-take,*
> *All of a maid without any make:*
> *Of all women she beareth the bell.*
> *Nowell, nowell, nowell . . .*

"It seems we have competition," the vicar remarked, redundantly, when the carol was over. "Time we moved on, I think." He chivvied the Scouts back into position, and the group slithered over the glistening sidewalk in the swinging yellow light of the vicar's lantern, which he bore before them on a pole. As they went they heard, apparently from the lane beyond the market, the baying of deep male voices, very loud, very confident.

"My word," Dad said, blandly, "the Boar's Head Carol. Haven't heard them singing that for years."

They stopped at the corner by the service station. " 'While Shepherds Watched,' " bellowed the vicar, so they sang it, while a single voice, sharp as splitting ice, cut through their chorus:

> *Gabriel from heaven-king*
> *Sent to the maiden sweet,*
> *Brought he this blissful tiding,*
> *And fair he gan her greet.*

"Move on!" the vicar shouted. "This is getting beyond a joke. Move on."

As they approached the deserted market square a light was seen, bobbing up Brewer's Street, above a cluster of dark figures.

"Could this be our friends, the Waits?" the vicar inquired, nastily, and raising his own lantern on its pole, he strode to meet his rivals, while the choir and the harmonium, conductorless, floundered through "See, Amid the Winter's Snow." Emma shuffled her cold feet in their cold boots and stopped singing to hear what would happen. One by one the rest of the choir fell silent as the vicar and the Waits met at last, outside Woolworth's.

"Merry Christmas," the vicar cried, not at all merry. The Waits stood and faced him, all in a lump. Their lantern shone over their heads, greenish, not glowing.

"I'm sorry it's come to a confrontation," said the vicar, "but we gave you plenty of warning. You were cordially invited to join us, and there were notices saying as much put up in the church porch, the post office, and outside the police station."

The leader of the Waits, a huge muffled man in a heavy coat, or cloak, stepped forward a pace, but still no one spoke. The vicar stepped back.

"We'd still be delighted," he said, less certainly, "if you'd care to join forces, but if not, I really must ask you to move on. It's not as if," he added, "you were even singing the same carols as us. Indeed," he went on, "I'm not sure that what you are singing *are* carols. I've never heard. . . ."

As one man, the Waits moved; forward, sideways, and disappeared. It looked very much as if they'd gone into Woolworth's, but that could not have been so, because Woolworth's closed at five-thirty, and it was now twenty minutes to nine.

"I think this has gone far enough," said the vicar, after an awkward silence. "A joke is a joke, but this is no joke. Who are they?"

"Well, we don't know any of them by name," Dad said. "We just call them the Waits. We always have."

"Since when?"

Mother broke in. "Since thirteen forty-eight, that's when."

"The year of the Black Death? This has been going on since *thirteen forty-eight?*"

"I did tell you it was a tradition," Dad said, self-righteously.

"You didn't tell me what kind of a tradition. Some of those carols are six hundred years old."

"So are the carol singers," said Mom.

There was a long pause. The Scouts hopped about on frozen toes.

"Nonsense," said the vicar, at last. "Carol singing as we understand it was unknown before the fifteenth century. How do you account for that?"

"They're a progressive crowd," Dad said. "They've picked up quite a lot of contemporary stuff since they d— since the Black Death. Jack Pewsey says he heard them having a go at 'In the Bleak Midwinter' last year—by Holst, you know. They don't really mind what they sing, as long as it's got a good tune. The true essence of carol singing, wouldn't you say?" he asked, with a mild smile.

Far away, from the general direction of Featherstone's Marine Diesels, came a last defiant burst of song.

> *Welcome be thou, heaven-king,*
> *Welcome, born in one morning.*
> *Welcome for whom we shall sing,*
> *Welcome Yule!*

There were no more carols that night. There was no more singing at all, but later, in the early hours of the morning, Emma was wakened by a fearful row coming from the streets outside. She went into her parents' room and found Mom and Dad in dressing gowns, standing by the window and looking down into the road.

155

"I could have told him this would happen," Dad said, as Emma crept alongside.

"Yes, but I notice you didn't," said Mom.

"No good flogging a dead horse," Dad said. "Still, he may pay attention next year. What on earth have they got down there?"

"Nothing on *earth*," said Mom.

"It sounds like iron kettles and ladles."

"I suppose it would be."

"Rough music."

Emma looked out into the street. In the moon's light she could see a steady surge of people passing by, silent themselves but raising a deafening clangor from pots and pans, tongs, hammers and billhooks that they carried.

"I think you'd better have another word with our Mr. Jarvis in the morning," Mom yelled, above the racket.

"D'you think it'll be necessary? After all, they've made their point. They've been carol singing for six centuries now. They're not going to stop because some hot-rod vicar tries to run Christmas like the Normandy landings."

"And warn him about Midsummer's Eve."

"Midsummer Eve's none of his business," said Dad, "or mine. Lord alone knows how long *that's* been going on."

Emma slipped back to her own room and lay listening to the Waits as they came down from Strang St. Thomas to play rough music around the vicarage until dawn broke on St. Thomas's Day. Through the clashing of iron on iron she heard voices raised, although she could not make out a tune. Whatever they were chanting, however, it was not a Christmas carol.